"Say," Doug said out of the blue. "Let me have your camera, will you?"

"Whatever for?"

"Just thought I'd take a picture of you in Hyde Park so you could send it to your folks."

Trish opened the case she'd toted along and handed him her Exacta. She felt a touch conspicuous, turning this way and that while he directed her moves and snapped photos. But at least she found consolation in knowing she'd be the one to develop them, in case she ended up looking as ill at ease as she felt.

Then, when she least expected it, Doug flagged down an unsuspecting passerby and asked him to take a couple frames of the two of them together. Just then a playful gust of wind tossed a tendril of Trish's hair over one eye, and Doug brushed it away with the backs of his fingers, sending quivery sensations spiraling to her toes. "Say cheese," he whispered nonchalantly into her ear as he moved in close for a final shot or two.

Trish couldn't help herself. She crossed her eyes and made a face instead. It was easier to clown around than to analyze the strange new yearnings being away from the office with Doug aroused within her.

SALLY LAITY has successfully written several novels, including a coauthored series for Tyndale, several Barbour novellas, and numerous Heartsongs. Most of her free time these days is spent trying to organize a lifetime of old photo albums and loose photographs into Memory Pages. Sally always loved to write; and after her four children were grown, she took college writing courses and attended Christian writing conferences. She has written both historical and contemporary romances and considers it a joy to know that the Lord can touch other hearts through her stories. She makes her home in Bakersfield, California, with her husband and enjoys being a grandma.

Books by Sally Laity

HEARTSONG PRESENTS

HP4—Reflections of the Heart
HP31—Dream Spinner
HP81—Better Than Friends
HP236—Valiant Heart
HP311—If the Prospect Pleases
HP355—Little Shoes and Mistletoe
HP423—Remnant of Forgiveness
HP511—To Walk in Sunshine

Don't miss out on any of our super romances. Write to us at the following address for information on our newest releases and club information.

Heartsong Presents Readers' Service
PO Box 719
Uhrichsville, OH 44683

Or visit www.heartsongpresents.com

Double Exposure

Sally Laity

Heartsong Presents

To Amanda Harris.
May God bless you always.

A note from the author:
I love to hear from my readers! You may correspond
with me by writing:

Sally Laity
Author Relations
PO Box 719
Uhrichsville, OH 44683

ISBN 1-58660-805-3

DOUBLE EXPOSURE

All Scripture quotations are taken from the King James Version of
the Bible.

All of the characters and events in this book are fictitious. Any
resemblance to actual persons, living or dead, or to actual events is
purely coincidental.

PRINTED IN THE U.S.A.

Note to Readers

The bombing raid over Germany portrayed in this story is fictional. The British stopped daylight bombing raids over Europe in 1941 because the high loss of bomber crews was unacceptable. Although American and British bombing missions took place in late 1942, the Americans restricted their attacks to targets in France. The Americans did not begin bombing Germany until 1943.

In researching *Double Exposure*, however, I found the history of the German resistance movement known as the White Rose utterly fascinating and decided to use it to motivate my fictional German characters.

The White Rose was a German student resistance movement against the government of Nazi Germany. Among its leaders were Hans and Sophie Scholl, a brother and sister who had been staunch members of Hitler Youth and the League of German Girls, programs designed to indoctrinate German young people with Nazi propaganda.

Over time, however, both Hans and Sophie became disillusioned with fascism. They heard rumors about concentration camps and saw friends punished for refusing to join Hitler Youth. When they learned that they could no longer read the works of German writers thought to be Jews, the Scholls became deeply disturbed.

After living through Kristallnacht, November 9–10, 1938, when German Nazis attacked Jewish people and property, damaging or destroying more than one thousand synagogues, vandalizing Jewish hospitals, homes, schools, and cemeteries, and killing at least ninety-one Jews, the Scholls rejected Nazi teachings.

When World War II broke out, Hans was studying medicine at the University of Munich. He discovered other young men who shared his sentiments: Hellmut Hartert, Christoph

Probst, Alexander Schmorell, and George Wittenstein. He introduced these friends to his sister when Sophie enrolled at the university in 1942.

Hans and his friends managed to obtain a duplicating machine and began printing leaflets that were distributed throughout the university and eventually to the rest of southern Germany. "Nothing is less worthy of a cultivated people than to allow itself to be governed by a clique of irresponsible bandits of dark ambition without Resistance," proclaimed the first pamphlet. The pamphlets quoted from German philosophers and encouraged Germans to sabotage the armaments industry. They criticized the war and the murder of Jews in Poland.

Resistance cells began to form in Berlin, Hamburg, and other large cities. From there the spirit of rebellion spread in all directions. The students ignored rumors that the Gestapo was planning to arrest them.

In February 1943, Sophie and Hans packed a suitcase with leaflets and took it to the university. The lecture rooms were to open shortly, so they deposited some leaflets in the corridors and disposed of the rest by letting the sheets fall from the top of the staircase to the entrance hall below. Before they could escape, the university's caretaker spotted them and seized them, notifying the Gestapo.

Hans and Sophie Scholl were arrested, along with their friend Christoph Probst. Within days the three were sentenced to death and were transferred to a large execution jail in München-Stadelheim. They were permitted to speak to their parents and later that day were executed by guillotine. Most of the other leaders in the group were arrested later and also executed.

But the White Rose lived on. Through it and other German resistance movements, the lives of countless Jews, Allied airmen, and soldiers were saved. Nor were the student leaders forgotten. Today a square at the University of Munich is named after Hans and Sophie Scholl, and the names of the Scholls and their friends have been given to streets, squares, and schools throughout the nation.

one

England, Summer 1942

Dusk faded swiftly in the mild, moonless night. Bumping northward along the undulating road from the seacoast town of Brighton in pitch darkness, the canvas-topped military truck rounded curves and crested hills at a fair clip. Tricia Madison marveled that the driver could find his way, given that the shielded headlights cast only narrow slits of downward-slanted light on the roadway ahead. Even as her weary mind wondered over his skill at driving in the blackout, the vehicle swerved as if to miss an obstruction or pothole in its path. A metal support banged against Tricia's head. She groaned and rubbed the sore spot.

"Got you, too, eh?" her uncle, sitting beside her, hollered above the racket of the engine. He clamped an empathetic hand on her knee. "Not to worry. For all our poor Britain's suffered during the bombing raids, she's nowhere near as bad off as Hitler might wish."

"Oh, really?" Tricia shifted to a more comfortable position on one of the hard seats running lengthwise down opposite sides of the lorry and turned to gaze uselessly out the back opening again. "I've been more than a little concerned about all that England has gone through as I read newspaper accounts back in the States. How about Gram's house, Uncle Sheldon? Is it still standing?"

"Couldn't say, Snooks. I haven't been over to the West Midlands for awhile to see for myself. But with Birmingham being a major producer in the aircraft industry, I know it's been targeted a number of times. Naturally Solihull and other surrounding towns have sustained their share of damage, too."

Drawing whatever limited comfort she could from the vague answer, Tricia sighed and reverted to silence. The noise of the motor precluded all hope of extended conversation anyway.

It had been years since she and her family had visited England, home of her great-grandmother. The frail old saint had passed on long ago. But Tricia had only to close her eyes to conjure up memories of endless rolling hills in variegated greens, charming hamlets with thatch-roofed cottages, and friendly souls who spoke very proper English, their accents falling like melodies on her ear.

Most of all, she'd been awed by the flowers. Seemingly everywhere, they spilled out of window boxes, climbed trellises, grew haphazardly in backyards, and adorned country gardens, lifting their bright faces to the sun in a glorious profusion of rainbow hues.

She and her daring older brother, Kendall, had loved scampering among the patchwork of hedgerows and stone walls. They had reveled in the curious thrill of touring majestic London and viewing the elaborate pageantry surrounding its elusive royal family. How special everything seemed, as if time had been suspended inside a real-life storybook.

But Ken would never see another changing of the guard. Tricia's throat tightened, and she swallowed hard. She couldn't let herself think about Kendall. Not now. Not yet. The grief was still too acute, almost more than she could bear.

Her uncle's booming voice brought a welcome distraction from her sadness. "Keep you waiting long in Lisbon, did they?"

"Seemed like forever," she yelled back, mentally reviewing the roundabout route she'd been forced to take because of the conflict. "With passengers rated by priority these days, I watched several planes take off before an extra seat turned up."

"Well, I'm just glad you finally made it. We'll sure appreciate another pair of helping hands, to say nothing of that keen eye of yours. We're trying to cover wartime life from as many angles as possible."

"I caught that great spread of yours in a recent issue of *Life* magazine. Superb cover photo."

"Some of my staff contributed shots," he admitted. "Don't know how all the other news agencies operate, but the guys who work for me help each other out a good part of the time, with cooperation running a close second to healthy competition. A major conflict provides plenty of news to go around. I'm just glad you were willing to come and work with us."

"How could I not?" For Tricia, the war had taken a very personal turn with the death of the brother she'd idolized all her life. He'd left California to join Britain's Royal Air Force over a year before America ever entered the conflict. Tricia knew there was no way to bring Kendall back, but she could help fight for the cause he believed in. Perhaps somehow, somewhere down the line, other sisters, other wives, and mothers would benefit.

Another sudden bump jolted Tricia awake. Realizing she must have dozed off, she turned to her uncle—anything to keep from giving in again to the exhaustion waiting to claim her. The sight of Sheldon Prescott's jovial face when she'd disembarked the plane had been most welcome. The khaki clothing he often wore to blend in with the military accented his big, solid frame, and somehow it suited his olive complexion and the dark hair only now beginning to show strands of silver at the temples. Now, however, she couldn't even make out his silhouette in the inky interior of the truck's canopy.

"I'm glad you were able to meet me, Uncle Sheldon. The airfield was teeming with people. I wouldn't have known how on earth to get to London at this late hour. I'd hoped to catch an earlier flight, but. . ."

He patted her knee again. "I've been keeping pretty close tabs on the birds coming in. I figured a seat would turn up for you eventually, so I just came here and waited. That way I could see you safely to the city."

"How's a newspaperman able to ride military vehicles?"

He laughed. "Oh, they're used to this ugly mug nosing

around for a story to send back home. I acquired clearance shortly after the press sent me here. And believe me, it wasn't hard convincing that kid at the wheel to let me pick up my pretty little niece, either."

Tricia smiled to herself. "Is it much farther?"

"Nope. Should be getting there directly."

Sure enough, the transport soon slowed to a stop and the engine was turned off. Tricia strained to see through the bowed opening but could make out nothing except more blackness.

"Better let me help you." Her uncle climbed over her, pausing to grab her bags before hopping out.

Tricia picked up the overnight case near her foot and looped the straps of her camera bag and purse over her shoulder. Then she stood and leaned into the older man's outstretched arms.

Once she actually set foot on the ground again, some indistinct shapes became visible—faint outlines of large buildings that barely stood out against the tiny stars in the midnight blue sky.

"Step lively," Uncle Sheldon quipped. "Or maybe I should say keep close. We'll soon have you settled for the night."

Enticing visions of a huge featherbed came unbidden to Tricia's mind, one as soft as the one in her bedroom at home. She imagined a soak in a hot bubble bath, perhaps a tall glass of lemonade to soothe her parched throat. But this was wartime, and gingerly navigating the unfamiliar, bomb-pocked sidewalk like a person without sight, she quickly let go of such impractical illusions. After three successive nights of sleeping sitting up in a cramped airport chair, a straw mat on a floor would do, if she could stretch out on it. Tomorrow she'd worry about comfort.

A piece of luggage in either hand, her uncle ushered her through both the massive revolving door of the multistoried Savoy Hotel and the heavy blackout drape hanging just inside.

For a second or two Tricia was blinded by light. But gradually, a splendidly decorated hotel lobby came into focus. Lovely. Luxurious. Bellmen in tuxedos. No straw mats here, she decided quite cheerfully, perusing gold-and-marble columns that accented the art deco interior. She hurried to catch up with her long-legged uncle, already headed for the registration desk.

Moments later they were ushered to a lovely suite as roomy and elegant as any she had ever stayed in. The blue walls framed in white moldings found their complement in the bedspread covering the vintage double bed, and the glow from matching lamps on the antique night tables bathed the whole room in warm welcome.

Uncle Sheldon tipped the bellboy, then set her luggage on the bed. "Sorry this isn't one of the suites overlooking the Thames, but at least you'll have a nice view of the courtyard in the daytime."

"It's fine. Better than I expected, to be honest."

He nodded. "They treat their customers well here." After a brief pause, he spoke again. "I've some friends in the city who've offered to billet you for as long as you're here. I'll take you there after you've settled into a routine. In the meanwhile, live it up. Just don't open the drapes at night."

"I don't suppose I dare consider drawing a bath," she ventured.

"Don't see why not, as long as you go easy on the water. The Savoy is pretty lenient. And they feed their customers extremely well—far better than the average Londoner, I might add. The other guys and I stay here most of the time ourselves. My room's on the next floor. Of course, if the air raid sirens kick on all of a sudden, we all hightail it down to the basement, where they have assigned mattresses for everybody."

"Is that a real possibility?" Tricia asked with a jolt of alarm.

"Naw. Not likely. The Germans are a little too occupied on the Russian front right now. They haven't bothered us for awhile."

His words soothed her. She smiled into his merry hazel eyes and moved to give him a parting hug. "Well, thanks again for meeting me and everything."

"Hey, nothing's too good for a fellow's favorite niece,

right?" He thumped her back, conjuring up a host of old memories. "See you bright and early, Snookums. Gotta register you with the police, get your picture taken, pick you up a ration book. . .all that rot. Then we'll head on down to Fleet Street, and I'll introduce you to the guys you'll be stuck working with." With that, he took his leave.

Automatically locking the door after her uncle, Tricia went right to the red-and-white marbled bathroom, so spacious it nearly matched her room for size. She ran only a few inches of luxurious bath water into the gleaming tub. She was too tired for a long soak anyway. While the tub filled, she unbuttoned her blouse and skirt and slipped them off. Peeling out of her slip and anklets, she realized how positively filthy she felt. A short while later, feeling clean and refreshed, Trish slipped between the sheets of the oh-so-comfortable bed and fell into a dreamless sleep.

અ

The morning dawned clear and summery, bringing memories of other perfect days Tricia had experienced in London. Dressing quickly before the mirrored bureau, she brushed her wavy, sable hair, using bobby pins to fasten the top and sides off her face in a soft roll. She then tied the back of her hair at the nape of her neck with a jade scarf that matched the green in her plaid skirt. She'd turned in all but one pair of stockings to the war drive back home but opted to risk getting a run on this her first day at her new job. After one last check to make certain the seams were straight, she slipped her feet into brown leather loafers, then went downstairs for breakfast.

Uncle Sheldon came striding into the hotel's coffee shop before she had half finished her bacon and eggs.

Nodding politely at a few other patrons in the elegantly furnished room whose taped and boarded windows were tastefully disguised by heavy drapery, he plunked himself down in a chair opposite hers and motioned to the waiter for coffee. "Say, you look a sight better than yesterday—not that you were bad off then, mind you." He gave a teasing wink.

Tricia grinned. "I can take the truth. After all those days in limbo, I resembled something the cat dragged in. But I slept like a baby last night." She paused. "Did you say the bombing raids stopped altogether? I was so tired I probably could have slept through anything."

His lips curved into a wry smile. "After seventy-six nights in a row of bombs raining down on us, Londoners aren't so complacent they think all the danger's past. The fire wardens still keep watch, folks stay on their toes, and everyone's careful about letting lights show at night. But right now the RAF is giving the Germans back some of what they gave us. Plus most of the Third Reich's forces are pounding Russia." His smile widened. "It's good you got some rest, though. You're in for a pretty full day."

Raising her cup to her lips, Tricia took a sip of her coffee.

Her uncle eyed her. "By the way, enjoy the coffee they serve here. Most places it tastes like shoe polish. Funny how our British cousins never figured out how to brew anything but tea, and even that's made it onto the ration list."

"I'll remember," she promised and savored each remaining mouthful.

" 'Ere you are, my good man," the crisply dressed waiter said pleasantly, delivering a cup filled with the steaming rich brew. "I say, will that be all?"

"Yes. Thanks." Uncle Sheldon turned to Tricia as the attendant strode away. "While we have a few minutes, why don't you bring me up to date on the latest from home? How are those parents of yours? Were they upset that I'd drag you out here into the fray?"

Upset! What an understatement. Tricia had no desire to describe that particular scene, with her elegant, always composed mother shocked speechless. Her father, distinguished and in control at all times, actually bellowed in outrage. Though Tricia understood their reactions, she had nevertheless held her ground. Eventually they'd relented. They always did. Being an only daughter had its advantages.

"They were hardly thrilled about it, to say the least. They would've preferred I stayed safe at home and got married, presented them with a passel of grandchildren."

"Not a bad plan. Any possibilities of that?"

"Marriage?" Tricia shook her head. "Later, maybe. I want to do something with my life first. Of course I had my hands full, convincing them I hadn't gone nuts by walking out on the job the *Chronicle* had offered covering the Little-Woman-Left-Behind-while-Hubby-Fights-for-Freedom bit. If you weren't here to look after me, they'd probably have chained me to a chair!"

A low chuckle rumbled from her uncle's chest.

"But they finally accepted my decision—even if they didn't quite agree with it. And, well, you know Daddy. Always blustering about, taking charge of things. He soon reverted to business as usual."

"Still a lot like his sister in that regard." Uncle Sheldon's eyes grew gentle with the mention of his own wife, left stateside.

"That reminds me. Auntie Maude sent you some socks and things. I'll get them when I've unpacked everything."

He nodded. "And how 'bout your mama?"

"She's doing fairly well, keeping up with her social engagements and relief work. Trying to stay busy."

"I. . .know it had to be rough on all of you, Kenny's plane getting shot up," he said soberly. "He almost made it back in that crippled crate, too. They were able to recover his body from the channel and give him a burial with full military honors, like they do for their own RAF boys. That was how he wanted things. When you feel up to it, I'll take you to see his grave, if you like."

Tricia struggled to breathe against the sting of unshed tears. She blinked quickly to regain her composure but could only smile her thanks. Kendall's death had been extremely difficult to accept; and though some individuals had tried to offer comfort through religious platitudes, she couldn't quite picture God as a loving, benevolent Father. To her He seemed distant and remote, and she had serious doubts He even knew about her, much less cared. She sloughed off the gnawing ache inside and forced a smile. "I don't know if I can handle that just yet, but thanks for the offer."

"Sure, Kid." He reached to give her hand a squeeze. "I understand. And there's someone else I know who'd like to meet you one of these days. A friend of his."

Too swamped by her sadness to acknowledge her curiosity, Tricia merely nodded.

Her uncle gulped the remainder of his coffee and, seeing that she had finished her meal, shoved back his chair and stood, dropping a few coins on the table. "Well, let's get going. We've got a lot of ground to cover today."

Tricia rose and retrieved the purse lying at her feet. Positioning the strap on her shoulder, she felt anticipation mounting at the thought of the new experiences awaiting her. How would this great, scarred city look in the harsh light of day?

She only hoped she had done the right thing in coming here.

two

Douglas St. Claire gently swished one more photo paper around in the developing solution and watched the image make a faint appearance before growing sharp and clear under the yellow safelight. Satisfied, he immersed it in the acidic short stop and fixing baths before washing it free of chemicals and placing it face up on an overturned tray. Once he squeezed the excess water from the print, he'd roll it face down on a blotter roll to dry overnight. Other shots from the previous day had already dried. Those he clipped to a thin wire strung above his worktable.

He'd been at this for hours, a fact that grated on him. All the other guys were out and about, tagging along with military personnel, photographing the action as it happened, documenting British sorties conducted in German-occupied France, and the success of RAF night bombing raids over Germany.

This can't be Your will for me, Lord. Stuck in this darkroom for a whole month when there's a war going on. I need to get back out there, do something. Stymied, he released a pent-up breath and stretched a kink out of his back before reaching for the next sheet.

He eyed the array of shots suspended before him. A few particularly brutal ones wouldn't pass the censor; but in years to come, when this struggle became history, it was likely that all of the photos would be published in one form or another. Meanwhile, once the military claimed the ones they wanted, he'd see that the Associated Press got its proper share of printable pictures and news copy.

If nothing else, being confined in solitude afforded him ample time to pray, and Doug used a lot of it for that purpose.

He envisioned his father's commanding presence in the pulpit of his church in Philadelphia, faithfully proclaiming the good news of salvation to an ever-diminishing flock, as members of the congregation were called away to help meet the increasing demands of war. No doubt his mother and sisters would be kept busy with relief efforts, aiding and comforting the bereaved families of the community, packing and sending boxes of necessities to local servicemen and the Red Cross.

But Doug's most fervent petitions always centered on his adventurous younger brother, Mike, a midshipman in the navy. He prayed constantly that God would surround the kid with His presence and keep him safe, wherever he was, in the fight for freedom from Axis tyranny.

Perusing yet another developing print, Doug's heart went out to the victims of the horrific scene, the families forever torn apart in a split second of destruction. He prayed they knew the Lord and could draw on His strength to get them through this cruel heartbreak. Such graphic photos were hard to dismiss from one's mind. He clipped it out of the way and went on to the next in the never-ending work pile.

❧

After her official registration as a visitor and newly arrived resident and news correspondent, Tricia found herself bicycling with her uncle around London on a pair of two-wheelers that had seen better days.

The horrendous damage wrought by German bombs throughout the city both stunned and appalled her. So many of the narrow streets and lanes had suffered unbelievable blows, obliterating entire blocks of buildings, leaving behind only grotesque, fire-blackened shells.

The saddest sights were the numerous majestic old churches that now lay in rubble, their once-graceful spires and magnificent grandeur reduced to a few crumbling sections of brick and stone standing roofless in eloquent muteness. In the gaping windows, twisted outlines of old leading dangled forlornly in vacant spaces once graced by exquisite stained glass.

Despite the cleanup efforts of industrious Britons, huge craters still rendered many streets impassible, and a number of sections remained unsafe to set foot in. "You say the area around the docks was the hardest hit," she mused.

"Yep. That and the East End. But amazingly, some of the most famous landmarks, like the Houses of Parliament, St. Paul's, the Tower of London, and Trafalgar Square, sustained only slight damage. A few were entirely untouched."

Tricia felt comforted at the sound of Big Ben bravely striking the hours and by the sight of the double-decker buses running more or less on schedule. Most city bridges remained in use, and stores conducted business even though their blown-out plate-glass windows remained boarded over. A faded sign in front of one of them, where the entire front had been eradicated, proclaimed itself MORE OPEN THAN USUAL in typically dry British humor.

Military vehicles of every shape and size overran the city; and service personnel flooded the streets, marching or sitting around waiting to be marched somewhere, their various uniforms indicating nationalities besides British. Many of the women sported smart uniforms as well. "Are there any actual civilians left in Great Britain?" Tricia asked just as a wolf whistle drifted her way.

Uncle Sheldon chuckled. "More than you might think. They do their part just like everyone else."

"But there are so few children." Where before she might have seen neatly dressed nannies pushing prams and strolling through the parks with two or three toddlers in tow, now only empty benches remained; and flowerbeds bloomed with no one to admire the vivid red and yellow roses.

"Most kids were taken out of harm's way at the beginning of the blitz," Uncle Sheldon explained. "Out to the country to stay with relatives—sometimes even strangers—or to be looked after by volunteer women's groups. As it turns out, though, now that Hitler's turned his attention away from the city, many parents have gone to reclaim their little ones. They figure if things heat up again and the worst happens, at least they'll all be together."

Tricia shuddered at the concept. "This is all so sad," she murmured. "So senseless."

Her uncle reached to give her hand an encouraging pat. "But they're a spirited lot, huh? Chin up, stiff upper lip, fix up, start over. After every bombing raid, folks banded together to make repairs, as if to prove that nothing Hitler threw at them would crush their spirit."

"It makes me proud to have such a courageous heritage behind me. What a blessing Great-grandmother Lillian was spared this grief. How unthinkably terrifying it must be to huddle helplessly in a shelter while destruction rains from the sky."

"If a person's lucky enough to reach one in time," the older man added.

Uneasy, Tricia stole a glance to the azure blue above, where silver barrage balloons resembling bloated whales still floated at various altitudes on steel tethers to discourage enemy planes from being able to fly low over the city.

Suddenly she braked to a stop. Having noticed the occasional waist-high post with a brass-colored sheet of metal on top, she had grown increasingly curious. "Exactly what are those things, Uncle Shel?"

"Gas detectors." He halted beside her. "If the Germans ever resort to using any of that, the metal will change color. That's why we get to lug these handy dandy babies everywhere we go." He tipped his head toward the cardboard gas mask case hanging on her handlebar.

Tricia would have preferred the dangling appendage to be her 35mm Exacta. But anticipating going to the headquarters of the newspapermen directly after registering, she had neglected to grab her camera bag. She couldn't believe it. Her first whole day here, wasted.

"Well, Snooks, what's say we pedal on over to Fleet Street and see who's manning our little store?"

Nodding in agreement as she took off after her spry uncle

again, Tricia tried to ignore the ache in her legs from the unaccustomed exercise. A break would feel incredibly welcome. She hoped Fleet Street wasn't much farther. To get her mind off her sore calves and thighs, she focused on the passing scenery.

Official shelter signs, black metal plates clamped to lampposts, dotted every block like street signs. Each one sported a small, inverted V-shaped roof to prevent the dim light from reflecting up into the night sky. Sandbags lay everywhere—at the base of every lamppost, lining buildings—some of them painted to match the structures.

An array of surface shelters lined the way. The long, windowless, flat-topped sheds built of tan bricks often abutted buildings. Some even ran right down the center of the streets. Notices tacked to them proclaimed SHELTER DURING BUSINESS HOURS or SHELTER FOR FIFTY PERSONS AFTER 5:00 P.M.

By the time Tricia and her uncle had reached the row of tall city buildings housing London's newspaper industry, she seriously doubted she'd be able to walk. But rather embarrassed that a man more than twice her age wasn't even winded, let alone limping, she suppressed any complaints and followed doggedly behind after parking the bikes, her muscles protesting every step.

When she and her uncle entered the structure the American press called headquarters, he waved Trish to the women's lavatory, while he took the men's. Even in the daytime, lights burned in the hallway, since the windows on the ground floor were taped haphazardly on the inside and boarded up on the outside.

"Our offices moved downstairs early on, for obvious reasons," Uncle Sheldon explained when she rejoined him. "Thought we'd wait awhile before moving back to the ground floor."

Already Tricia could hear the steady *tap-tap* of typewriter keys and the intermittent end-of-line bells. With each step, the sounds grew louder. Reaching the landing, her uncle opened the door and gestured for her to enter.

She had no idea so many desks and filing cabinets could be crammed into one room. At the occupied stations, a handful of individuals busily pecked away at their Remingtons and Royals.

"Hi, all," Uncle Sheldon hollered. The typing ceased. "I'd like to introduce my niece, Tricia Madison, just arrived from stateside to help us out."

"Cheerio, Miss," someone called out, followed by an assortment of other friendly words that put Tricia at ease, despite the head-to-toe once-overs and the significant glances the men swapped with one another.

"You shouldn't have to take much guff from this bunch," Uncle Sheldon said out of the side of his mouth. "Anybody who gives you trouble will have to answer to me. Over there," he said, indicating the farthest desk, "is Paul. Then Babs, Dora, and Ned. We'll worry about tacking on all their last names later."

"Hello, everyone," Tricia offered, sure it would not take long for her to connect the right name to the proper face.

"Welcome aboard," one of them called.

Her uncle kneaded his chin. "Hm. Doug's not around. Must be in the darkroom. This way."

Tricia saw a red light burning above the door they were approaching. For a second, she almost expected her uncle to barge right in, but he merely rapped.

The light went out almost at once. The door opened, and a tall, sandy-haired man emerged.

Tricia's gaze rose to meet a pair of arresting, wide gray eyes set in an open, honest face with a square chin and obvious five-o'clock shadow. The broad shoulders weren't exactly lost on her, either; nor was his nonchalant stance. He wore a canvas work apron over his trousers and white shirt; and beneath his rolled-up sleeves, strong forearms sported fine blond hair.

A toothy grin made its way across the man's mouth.

"Doug." Uncle Sheldon clamped a hand on the fellow's

shoulder. "My niece just arrived from stateside. Tricia Madison. Tricia," he said, turning to her, "meet Douglas St. Claire, our newest correspondent for the Associated Press and all-around good Joe." He winked.

Tricia realized she was still staring. She pressed her lips together and offered a hand. "Pleased to meet you." Surely it was her imagination that his big hand held hers a fraction longer than necessary.

"Ditto. Come to take in England's once-fair sights?" Doug waggled uneven brows in a comical fashion as he casually draped an arm around her shoulders.

Something about his manner—to say nothing of his familiarity—miffed Tricia. She shrugged the offending member from her person and tried for her iciest tone. "Actually, no. I'm here to work."

"Ah. Right," he said with a measure of chagrin and cast an embarrassed look at Uncle Sheldon. "In that case, I extend my warmest welcome to you, Tricia Madison." He tipped his head in utmost respect.

Now she felt completely confused. Was the guy the fresh type or wasn't he? She'd give him the benefit of the doubt. For now.

Either way, it made no difference, since the two men launched into a business discussion as if she weren't even there. She wandered a few steps away and idly surveyed the place, the desks piled to the hilt with stacks of papers and file folders, a raft of maps and charts lining the walls. Despite the chaotic appearance, it radiated a decidedly efficient air. No one seemed to be lazing around. Not spotting any vacant workstations, she wondered exactly what her duties would entail.

"Yeah, I just decided to close up shop for the day when you knocked," she heard Doug St. Claire say. "I can show her the ropes first thing in the morning."

"Great. Well, then, we'll be off, too. See ya tomorrow." Motioning for Trish to precede him, Uncle Sheldon pointed her toward the exit.

But the entire way out, she was more than conscious of one particular pair of eyes following her.

❧

Idiot! Doug railed inwardly as he went to his desk and grabbed what he wanted to take to his hotel room for the night. He had no idea what had possessed him to act in such a forward manner toward Tricia Madison. Chalk it up to weariness or being cooped up too long in the dreary confinement of the darkroom; but no matter the reason, he had managed with typical aplomb to get himself off on the wrong foot with her. Seemed he possessed a rare talent for making a bad first impression, particularly when it came to beautiful women.

He let out a silent whistle. She sure was a looker, with that glorious, shiny hair, those huge blue-green eyes, features as delicate and feminine as his younger sister, Ruthie's. She probably was some guy's sister, too. Why had he been such a jerk? Well, he'd apologize to her first chance he got, and hopefully that'd be the end of it.

What a relief, though, to have someone to take over that tedious darkroom work. Now he wouldn't be pulled out of action for a month at a time whenever his turn came up for that chore. He could get back to covering the war. Thinking how Tricia had set him and the other fellows free, he could just about kiss her. If he was that kind of guy. Which, of course, he wasn't; nevertheless, a slow smile insisted on creeping across his mouth.

"What's so funny?" slick-haired Paul Reynolds asked from the paper-strewn desk next to Doug's. He removed the pencil from behind his ear and stuck it in the top drawer.

"Nothing," Doug assured his curious coworker. "Nothing at all. In fact, things are finally beginning to look up, my friend." Gathering his belongings, Doug strode, whistling, to the door.

three

Gradually relinquishing sleep the next morning, Tricia yawned and stretched luxuriously in the comfortable hotel bed. Then she remembered. This day would mark the beginning of her personal campaign to support the war effort!

Until now she'd only been able to envy her college sorority sisters who'd gotten involved in some venue of service for their country after the bombing of Pearl Harbor. One had stepped right into the army's nursing corps. Another acquired a job in the Office of Strategic Services. Tricia's very best friend, multi-talented Katherine Montgomery, had found her niche in the USO, keeping up the morale of homesick young men.

But I'm finally part of things, too! Tricia affirmed with a smile. Even if the devastation caused by the incessant German bombing raids around Britain had been photographed and documented to the point of redundancy, there had to be something she herself could record on film. Something. . .human. An angle the average person anywhere might relate to. And whatever it was, she intended to find it. And to see that Germany got what was coming to it, as well.

Thinking of her parents and Kate, so far away, Tricia wished she were a praying person. But if prayers really helped, an inner voice reasoned, why were so many fine young men and women being maimed for life or snuffed out entirely? It made no sense.

Obviously, the unanswerable would not be solved by lying in bed all day. Time to dress for work—and today she wouldn't forget her Exacta! Before donning a rust linen skirt and white blouse, she made certain the camera bag had a good supply of film and flashbulbs. Then she went to freshen up.

When Tricia arrived at the newspaper office, she found her

brawny uncle already there. Lounging against a filing cabinet, his suit somewhat rumpled, his tie loosened, he held a mug of coffee in hand as he chatted with the other staff members.

"That's my gal," he boasted loud enough for the whole world to hear. "First day on the job, and already we can set our watches by her."

" 'Cause the babe knows this is where the real action is," ruddy-complexioned Ned teased, a flirtatious glint in his dark blue eyes. He filled a cup with coffee from a pot sitting on a hot plate in the corner and brought it to her, his gaze drinking her in from head to toe, obviously liking what he saw. "Welcome to the party. Ned Payne's the name. Swell to have you aboard. Last time I was the one who pulled dark-room duty."

"Thanks, Ned." Unsure whether or not to take offense from his somewhat forward manner, Tricia accepted the hot drink, puzzling over his last statement before trying a cautious sip.

The girls rose from their desks and walked toward her, friendliness pervading their smiles. The shorter one, slightly plump with a reddish bob and a bumper crop of freckles, spoke first, her British accent in evidence.

"Jolly good to have you with us. I'm Barbara Crandall— Babs to my friends. Besides trying my utmost to keep these wild lads in line, I keep the books and files, plus do any extra typing that needs done."

"And I'm Dora Swain." Slender and blond, with chin-length hair in soft waves, the stylish young American woman smiled a polite greeting as she offered her hand. "I freelance, covering subjects of special interest to women for the AP. Hope you like working here."

Trish relaxed a notch. "So far I do."

"Take it from me, Doll," Ned piped in, "we promise not to let you get bored."

A collective chuckle made the rounds as he did an about-face and sauntered to his desk.

Babs gave Tricia a gentle nudge in the ribs with her elbow

and spoke in a conspiratorial tone. "Don't let the drip get to you, Luv. He thinks he's the Almighty's gift to women, does our Ned, and rather lives up to his name. But we've learned to ignore him."

"Where are you staying?" Dora asked.

"Presently at the Savoy. But my uncle says he's arranged other more permanent quarters for me. I'm not sure where, yet."

"Well, you just let Dora or me know if you need anything," Babs said. "You'll find us at our desks, rain or shine, you will."

"Thanks, I'll remember that." Watching after them as they returned to their stations, Tricia noticed that the British girl's clothing, though clean and neatly pressed, showed obvious wear. Surmising that most Londoners' resources went to obtaining food and keeping up repairs rather than splurging on fashions, she sought her uncle's attention.

A big smile crinkled the lines on his broad face as he hastened to her side. "Anxious to get started, huh? Well, now that you've made a few friends here, we'll get down to business. You do know your way around a darkroom, right?"

"Yes." A niggling dread inched up her spine.

"Good. Good. The guys have been on my back about being pulled away from the action for extended periods every time their turns come up. I figured since you majored in journalism and photography, you'd be just the one to fill that spot, let them get back to the war coverage."

"I'm. . .here to take over the darkroom?"

"You got it, Snooks," he replied, as if the mere suggestion was the fulfillment of her dreams.

"But. . .you said I'd get to take pictures." She hoped her voice didn't sound brassy, but this news caught her off balance. Way off balance.

"And you will, you'll see. You don't work on weekends, you know, plus most of us head home every day at four o'clock. With England on double summer time—that is with the clocks moved ahead two hours for the duration of the war to take advantage of daylight—that leaves plenty of time for you to do your own thing."

Tricia's spirit took a nosedive. She hadn't had the slightest inkling she'd be stuck in a dreary basement darkroom day in, day out, when there was so much of life-and-death importance happening all over the British Isles. But apparently this was to be her lot in this war, like it or not. As that bleak reality settled over her, she pressed her lips tightly together to keep from saying something that wouldn't exactly honor her elder.

"Cheerio," a happy voice called out just then, and Douglas St. Claire entered, crossing the room in a few confident strides. "Ah, our new gal is here, I see."

Rooted to the floor in mild shock, Tricia remained motionless as her gaze swung his way. She stared askance at him, too distressed to acknowledge his arrival. On the edge of her vision, she also caught Dora Swain's attention riveted to the tawny-haired newsman, the attractive woman's interest plain to see.

But Doug seemed oblivious to the rest of the staff as he approached Tricia and her uncle. "And an eager beaver she is, too," he quipped. "Come on, Tricia. I'll show you the ropes."

Glumly, she followed. On the way, her shoulders drooped, and the camera bag slipped off and snagged on her arm.

૨૪

Doug couldn't help noticing that the spark that had been in Tricia Madison's expressive turquoise eyes when they'd met the day before had dimmed considerably. Even so, she granted him her full attention while he rattled off the pertinent details regarding procedures established long before her presence graced this dull workroom. She appeared to be filing away in her mind the information on the various supplies, the daily routine, and the order of things, complete with whys and hows.

"And we use different color clips to fasten the finished photos," he said, "according to their owners. That way, each guy can claim what's his. Red for Ned's—figured that'd be easy to remember—blue for Paul's, green for your uncle's—"

"Yellow for yours, I suppose?" Tricia snapped, breaking in on his long-winded discourse.

Doug stopped talking and leaned his elbows on the elevated worktable, positioning his head on a level nearer hers. He smiled gently. "You're not too keen on all this, are you?"

"What gives you that idea?" she asked, not meeting his gaze.

"Oh, I don't know. The way you're fiddling with those loose hairs, maybe, twisting them within an inch of their life. The way your eyebrows dip into that V above that cute nose of yours. The way—"

She let go of the strand of hair and scrunched her nose in disgust. "Look, Mr. St. Claire."

"Doug."

She huffed and started again. "Look, Doug. This isn't exactly what I expected, know what I mean? But I told Uncle Sheldon I'd come and help out. So that's what I'll do. Maybe in time I'll grow to be thrilled about it, I don't know. But for now, would you just. . .just—"

He held up a hand. "Enough said. I'll get out of your way and try not to pester you. But just so you know, this little back-room job you seem to consider so mundane is quite the opposite. You don't have any idea how much we guys appreciate having you here so we don't have to lose valuable time out in the field. In fact, we were ecstatic to hear you were coming. Who knows? I might be able to figure out a way to make up for your disappointment. Then maybe you'll find some good reasons for having given up life in the States for this common, unglamorous, everyday job that needs somebody—with considerable talent, I might add—to do it."

Her eyes rose to his. Beautiful, they were. Eloquent and wide, with an odd vacant quality to them. . .and a whole lot of sadness. "I doubt it," she said flatly, "but thanks anyway."

Undaunted, he plunged on. "Well, as the Bible says, 'All things work together for good.' Maybe the Lord has His own reasons for sending you here. If so, they'll be evident in time, I'm sure."

An incredulous smile quivered over her lips. "You actually believe all that religious stuff?"

"Sure do. Believe it, live by it, rest on it, and love doing so, to boot."

Tricia merely shook her head. "Funny, I never would have suspected you of being a churchy guy when we were introduced."

Doug felt heat rise from his shirt collar and continue up over his ears at the memory of how brash and ungentlemanly he must have seemed to her. He cleared his throat. "Yeah, I know. I acted like a royal cad, didn't I? I was only trying to be friendly, but it sure must not have appeared that way to you. I can only apologize and hope you won't hold it against me forever."

She seemed to consider his words, then shrugged. "I guess we all act out of character once in awhile." The hint of a smile tugged at the corner of her rosy lips as she slowly raised those long lashes and looked directly at him. "Normally I'm not this miserable myself. And. . .I'm sorry, too."

Doug flashed her a grin and straightened to his normal stance. "Hey, no problem. Sounds like what we've got here is a truce. And believe me, I'm not gonna waste it." He paused to switch gears before the chance to pick up the earlier subject vanished, to be lost for good. "But getting back to what I was saying, it wouldn't surprise me if, one of these days, you come to feel the same way about the Lord yourself. A war has a way of changing a person's outlook on life."

She didn't miss a beat. "I wouldn't hold my breath, St. Claire."

Nodding, Doug moved to the door. He wanted to say more. He had the feeling that the profound emptiness in Tricia's eyes stretched all the way down into her soul. But he knew that before she would ever be receptive to anything that would feed such heart hunger, he needed to do some serious praying, give God time to prepare the way. "If you have any questions or need anything, give a holler," he said then left the darkroom.

❧

Red for Ned, green for Uncle Shel, Tricia mouthed mockingly, as the door closed after Doug. Gratified by his apology, she was glad she had followed with her own. But that didn't lessen the anger she felt over having been banished to this dungeon. If only Uncle Sheldon had prepared her for it, maybe she wouldn't have had her heart so set on making her own mark in the male-dominated world of photojournalism. In any case, she needed time to get used to her disappointment. She'd adjust, more's the pity, and would do her best. But a good long while would pass before she'd like it.

Above all else, she concluded with a scathing look at her surroundings, the work area needed to be neat and well organized. This place obviously had been a man's domain, with things piled about without apparent reason or system. Were all the guys this disorganized in everything they did? Well, regardless, this was her hill to conquer now. And she would have it set to rights before the day was over.

After restoring as much order as possible in the darkroom's limited confines, Tricia fastened a heavy work apron over her clothing to protect it from the caustic chemicals she'd be using, then checked the levels of the developing baths and eyed the baskets of work waiting for her. A resigned sigh emerged. At least she'd be busy and wouldn't have to be watching a clock.

Soon she had an impressive number of finished prints drying on the blotter, with others pegged on the wire. And every one of them appeared nothing short of incredible. Many had been snapped on the fringes of battle, where it was unlikely she'd ever get to go. The Associated Press employed no small array of talent.

Public concern in Britain had shifted from the critical Russian front to the Eighth Army's struggle to stop Rommel's push toward Egypt, and the photographs proved that the RAF was continuing to batter Germany's production bases. Tricia wondered if all the foreign correspondents in this office were afforded the same clearance as Uncle Sheldon. Did they fly in the military planes and march with the troops into combat? If so, the news staff would face the same danger of being felled by a bullet or a grenade as the lowliest private. The dire thought weighed heavily on her mind. She knew Auntie Maude pictured Uncle Sheldon holding down a desk inside some safe, out-of-the-way building in London that no bombs could possibly penetrate.

And what about Doug? Was there someone in particular who worried after his welfare? A sweetheart back in the States, perhaps, waiting and praying for his safety? Certainly a guy as manly—face it, gorgeous—as he must have a whole fan club in his hometown.

Tricia smiled wryly. Too bad he had to spoil all that charm by being so religious. She was used to wolf whistles, and what fellow didn't flirt outrageously around anything in a skirt? But having some guy spewing forth a string of high and noble platitudes at her would be another matter entirely.

Oh, well. She had other things on her mind. Other plans. She had come to England for two reasons: first, to support the Allied cause against the people who had murdered Kendall, and second, to establish her name as a respected photojournalist. That's precisely what she would endeavor to do, despite being cooped up in this darkroom. Nothing and no one—not her uncle and especially not somebody as handsome as Douglas St. Claire—would sidetrack her from that dream.

four

Tricia smiled as she and her uncle approached the charming, two-story London home with its ivy-covered stone exterior. At any other time it might have done as a picture postcard, framed by trees and neat hedges, with bountiful rose bushes on either side of the entrance. But as they parked their bikes and strode up the stones bisecting the front path, her gaze shifted to the partially crumbled far wall. The pocked ground beside it and the rubble beyond revealed the complete destruction of a neighboring house and a few others in the area as well.

She swallowed hard.

Despite the scars of war made all the more dreary by a somber gray sky, the sweet perfume of the roses mingled with the scent of moist earth in the determined optimism so typical of the British spirit.

The door opened before Uncle Sheldon had a chance to knock. He doffed his cap and held it in his hands.

"Oh, you've come," a pleasant-faced woman said in a well-modulated voice, her regal height and bearing, qualities that would set her apart under any circumstances. She smiled at them, her close-set blue eyes shifting from Uncle Sheldon to Tricia and back in friendly appraisal. Side-parted brown hair, fashioned into a tight roll at the neck, bore a light sprinkling of silvering strands against her crisp white blouse and tailored skirt.

"Sure have, Isabel. Thought I'd bring by my niece, Tricia Madison. Tricia, I'd like you to meet Isabel Wyndham, a gracious lady and friend to all. Seems the lot of us have enjoyed her generous hospitality on numerous occasions. A finer cook you'll never find. Nor a sweeter soul, for that matter. She even provides us with a special-interest story upon occasion."

A soft blush tinted the patrician cheeks, accenting the lines that tension and anxiety had carved in the woman's delicate skin. Her eyes held a haunted quality, as if they'd seen far more than she might have wished.

"I'm very happy to meet you, Mrs. Wyndham," Trish said, returning the smile of welcome that had yet to dim.

"Oh, we'll have none of that, now. 'Tis Isabel I am to my friends, and Isabel I'll be to you. Tricia, is it? Well, come in, come in. We'll have us a spot of tea while we visit. I've a smidgeon put by for special occasions."

"Thank you." At Uncle Sheldon's gesture for her to precede him, Tricia stepped into the homey entry. Its welcoming air brought pleasant memories of her late grandmother's cottage.

Their hostess ushered them to the parlor, where they settled into worn, overstuffed chairs. Tricia tried not to stare at the one badly damaged wall, temporarily patched with boards. A collage of embroidered samplers did its part to make the repairs seem less stark. She averted her eyes.

Moments later, Mrs. Wyndham returned to the room, bearing a tray of refreshments. She set it on a cherry lamp table, then poured and served the tea. "The scones won't be very sweet, I'm afraid, what with the sugar ration and all. . . ."

Uncle Sheldon brushed her apology aside with a wave of a hand. "This is fine, dear lady. And neither of us takes sugar in our tea."

She handed the cups around, keeping the last for herself, pouring a dab of milk from a cream pitcher first, then filling her cup with the rich brew. "Took me awhile to get used to it so plain, 'tis a fact, but I find I'm minding it less and less. And we do save the milk ration for our tea."

"Wilfred's not at home?" Uncle Shel dunked his scone, then bit off the moistened chunk.

"No, he's off on fire warden duties just now. Truth is, he finds plenty to do from day to day, does my Will, with the warden business and repair work."

"As I'm sure you do yourself," Uncle Sheldon added. "Seems the hard work you do serving those canteen meals might be better left to...well, younger women, you might say."

"They've nearly all been called up, you see. But one does what one can. Especially when there are so many in need, so many who've been bombed out of their homes." She took a sip.

Munching her own flaky biscuit, Tricia felt aware of her hostess's gaze and looked up to meet it.

"You must be the younger sister Kenny spoke of so fondly," Isabel said. "I recognize you from the photograph he carried. All of us were saddened at his loss. A fine lad, was our Kendall. A fine, fine lad."

"Thank you," Tricia murmured. "I didn't realize you knew my brother."

"Ken made many friends here," Uncle Sheldon said. "No doubt Isabel will share some of her memories with you in the future. She's offered to billet you as long as you're in London. She and her husband feel that being with a family will be less impersonal for you than staying on indefinitely at the Savoy. To say nothing of sparing you considerable extra expense."

"How very kind of you." Tricia offered her a smile.

" 'Twill be our pleasure," she returned. "Having a young person around again will make up for our daughter's absence. Margaret took a post with the Women's Auxiliary Air Force up north some time ago. We don't get to see her often now, perhaps once a month or so. Truth is, I think she finds it difficult to spend much time in the city. Too many reminders of times past."

Tricia nodded. She had the odd feeling that Mrs. Wyndham was on the verge of saying more, but Uncle Sheldon cleared his throat and met the woman's eyes. She returned her attention to her tea.

Puzzled, Tricia only half-listened to the two as they drifted into a discussion regarding the current state of London and the rate of progress in the way of ongoing repairs.

"So it'll be a frightfully long time before our lovely church is actually rebuilt, if ever," Isabel commented wistfully.

"I wouldn't doubt it." Uncle Sheldon set aside his empty cup and stood, nodding to Tricia to join him. "Well, we do thank you for the visit and the refreshments, Isabel. Now that you and my favorite niece have met, I'll see about bringing her belongings up here on Saturday, if that suits you. We'll keep her at the hote 'til then."

"As you wish. I shall set Margaret's room to rights for her stay."

"You're certain I won't be a bother?" Tricia asked, suddenly feeling the intruder.

"Not at all, not at all. My husband and I shall love having you here. And when Margo pops in for a visit, she'll be glad there's someone her age to talk to, I'd wager."

"Now that the matter's all settled," Uncle Sheldon began, "we'll be off. Thank you again, Isabel."

"You're welcome. I'll see you both on the week's end, then."

He nodded and donned his hat, then strode down the path.

Tricia cast a backward glance toward the house as she mounted her bicycle and caught the older woman's pensive expression. She smiled in farewell, receiving an answering smile and wave before pedaling after her uncle.

"How did you meet Mrs. Wyndham?" she asked, catching up to him.

"Through Kenny. He made quite a few friends, being with the RAF."

Tricia shrugged. "I can't help feeling I'll be an imposition on the Wyndhams. After all, what if their daughter is upset when she comes home and finds an interloper in her room?"

"She won't. She's not like that."

"You know their daughter?"

"Yep. Margo's every inch as sweet as her mom. She's suffered some tough losses in the blitz herself, among her coworkers and close friends. I'm sure you'll take right to her when she comes around. Besides, the Wyndhams can use your help. The extra rations, you know. Like so many other Britons, they suffered tremendous financial losses because of the war."

"I never thought about that. If I can help out, then of course I'll stay with them."

"And you can keep the bike. It'll make it easier for you to get to work every day. That way when it rains, you'll only get half as wet as you would if you had to walk the whole distance."

Tricia peered up at the heavy clouds. "Which shouldn't be far off. Looks like it'll douse us any second."

"Well, this is London," he reminded her. "We get as much rain as sun."

"So I remember."

The ensuing showers that began that afternoon and lasted throughout the next two days barely affected Tricia. Darkroom duties gave her little time to be out in the elements; and having resigned herself to her fate, she settled quickly into a comfortable, if tedious, routine.

"Hmm. Pretty impressive work," Doug commented when he dropped off some film late one afternoon as Tricia bustled about setting the place in order for the weekend.

She paused in restocking the shelves with supplies from cartons and turned to see which pictures held his interest. "Oh, those. Uncle Sheldon took them yesterday when he interviewed some RAF pilots after a bombing mission." Unconsciously, she moved closer to study them herself. "For such young men, they seem older than they really are. Something about their eyes, I think." Then, realizing he'd probably scorn her silly opinions, she quickly resumed her task.

But surprisingly, Doug didn't make the snide comments she'd braced for.

Tricia glanced his way and found those perceptive gray eyes regarding her. "What, do I have my apron on inside out or something?"

"Nope. Not at all. I was thinking about what you said. I've often admired RAF pilots. Those guys have seen more than their share of war's horrors. Lost members of their squadrons, their best friends." He paused. "Are you doing anything tomorrow?"

"Excuse me?"

"Thought you might like to go on a photo excursion. I know a few places you'd probably find interesting. As I recall, I did say I'd try to make up for your being stuck in the darkroom."

Tricia had to smile. "I'm touched, St. Claire. I really am. But alas, I'm moving out of the Savoy in the morning. Uncle Shel is taking me to stay with a family who's offered to billet me. So I'll be visiting with them and getting settled in."

"You don't say. Where?"

She frowned. "Funny, with all the road and street signs taken down, I'm not really sure. I never thought to ask the address."

"Oh. Too bad. Well, another time then. Though what you'll find to photograph that no one has already done is a mystery. See you around, Tricia." And with that, he took his leave.

Tricia stared after him momentarily. She hadn't believed he'd been serious about that offer, but apparently he kept his word. One point in his favor. He was turning out to be quite an enigma. And she did feel there had to be something fresh to focus her efforts on. No matter what he or anyone else said to dissuade her, she would find it.

The next morning, she packed all her belongings and had her luggage taken down to the lobby in readiness for her move. It would be some time before she'd enjoy such elegance and comfort again, she realized, sweeping a last look around the suite she'd called home for almost a week. She was no stranger to such opulence, but she also knew it would be much easier to relate to the war-weary Britons once she lived as they did.

She went to meet her uncle for breakfast and take advantage of the sumptuous fare provided by the Savoy one last time. Then she helped him load her things into a borrowed Jeep so they could drive to the Wyndhams'.

When they arrived, Isabel threw the door wide and smiled, coming out to meet them. "I heard you coming."

"I don't doubt it," Uncle Sheldon said, climbing from the

vehicle and grabbing Tricia's bags from the backseat.

"And we're so glad to have you, my dear." The older woman came to Tricia's side, British reserve restraining her from offering more than a smile. "We've got your room ready."

"I know you and Wilfred will take good care of her," Uncle Sheldon said before Tricia could utter a word.

"Not just us," she said, her smile widening. "Margaret's come home. She's got a few days' leave."

A pang of nervousness shot through Tricia at the thought of meeting the young woman whose bedroom she'd be usurping. She cut a glance to her uncle.

"Well, I'll be!" he exclaimed with an ear-to-ear grin. "Isn't that the best news!"

At the sound of his booming enthusiasm, a slender, golden-haired English beauty stepped into view. Her rosy lips curved into a smile, and she flew to him. "Sheldon Prescott. How very chipper you look!"

He dropped Tricia's bags and gave her one of his trade-mark hugs. "Not half as wonderful as you do, Margo. How've you been?"

"I'm getting by. . .but just barely." A saucy wink and her light tone belied her answer.

"Well, I've brought someone to meet you," he said, releasing her. "This is my niece, Tricia Madison. Your mum and dad have been kind enough to offer your room to her."

"I. . .hope you don't mind, Miss Wyndham," Tricia stammered, moving a step nearer.

"Mind? I've been wanting to meet you forever," she said. "And do call me Margo. Your brother told me all about you. Do you mind if I call you Trish?"

"No, not at all." Immediately warming to the daughter of the house—another person who'd known Kendall—Tricia's former reservations vanished. Maybe it wouldn't be so bad here after all. . .wherever here was. She'd have to inquire about the address. Just in case Doug St. Claire felt inclined to take her on one of those photo excursions he'd mentioned.

five

"And no tour is complete without visiting the Anderson shelter," Margo gushed dramatically, after setting Tricia's belongings in her room and escorting her through the remainder of the house. "They're all the rage. So frightfully stylish, just everyone has one."

"Yes, I've heard of them," Tricia said, following the young woman outside to the backyard, where a sizeable vegetable garden dominated a good portion of ground. Already at ease in the unpretentious girl's presence, Tricia enjoyed Margo's cheerful banter, finding it a delightful change from the solitude of the hotel room.

"Well, this is it," Margo said airily as the two of them approached what appeared to be a half-above-ground cellar formed of walls of sheet iron and heavily banked on the outside with dirt. "Come along. You need to experience the full effect." She opened the small door and bent to enter, her shoulder-length blond pageboy falling forward with her movements.

The limited amount of daylight coming through the opening, aided by the flickering glow of an oil lamp Margo lit, illuminated a dreary enclosure scarcely large enough to house three cots, a small table, and crates of supplies on shelves against one wall. "Of course, it's miserably cramped when we're all inside the thing," she admitted. "Water seeps up through the floor when it rains; and if it's cold enough to require heat, one could quite easily suffocate."

"But it's safe during bombings?" Tricia asked, glancing uneasily about the bleak shelter.

"More or less. A direct hit would rather demolish it, of course. But otherwise, it can deflect flying shrapnel. Fortunately there hasn't been much need for these of late, but likely they'll remain for the duration." She extinguished the lamp, and they returned to the house.

To Tricia's relief, Uncle Sheldon accepted an invitation to stay for supper. His presence did much to ease her transition into the home, making her feel less like a stranger when the family gathered around the linen-covered table in the dining room. She recognized the quality of the heirloom mahogany furniture with its handsome matching buffet and felt a wave of sadness at deep scratches that had been polished over, possibly from flying debris during an air raid.

Wilfred Wyndham, Margo's father, said a brief prayer of thanks over the meal. Rail-thin, with a prominent nose and a pronounced overbite, he had merry blue eyes that held a glint of suppressed humor as he ladled out bowls of steaming vegetable soup at the head of the table and passed them around. "I say, Tricia, are you encountering problems finding your way round the city since your arrival? We've lost a number of our most familiar landmarks, to say nothing of the missing street signs."

She paused in buttering a warm roll Margo had offered her. "I had a real problem at first, but I pay very close attention when I'm out and about. It was shocking to see the extent of the damage everywhere."

"Quite. But we're setting things to rights a bit at a time."

"I doubt London will ever regain its former glory," Margo said dryly. "What a loss of our heritage, when the very heart of our historic publishing industry burned to ashes. So many of Sir Christopher Wren's magnificent churches and other grand old buildings are no more."

"But Britain hasn't lost her spirit," Uncle Sheldon commented. "That's what counts most. It's the spark of life that'll help her overcome even this devastation, given time."

" 'Tis all we've had," Isabel said on a somber note. "Spirit. I doubt Hitler realized how very close he came to breaking it. If the bombing raids had continued another few days or—heaven forbid—weeks, that would've been the end of us, 'tis a fact."

"Well, no doubt the Lord had a hand in that," Wilfred chimed in. "He looks after His own, strengthens the side of the right. Otherwise, why would the bombings have ceased at the very moment when they'd surely have finished us?"

More churchy people, Tricia conceded, focusing on the soup, tasty despite the absence of meat. Not only would she be enduring endless religious clichés from Doug St. Claire, but likely from her host family as well. What had she done to deserve this? She maintained an expression she hoped was neutral enough not to reveal her displeasure. Besides, now that America had entered the war, these well-intentioned people would realize soon enough whose efforts would ultimately bring the Third Reich to its knees. God would have nothing to do with it.

"If no one wants more soup," her hostess announced, "we'll have our dessert now. Margaret, Dear, would you help?"

"Of course." Placing her napkin on the table, Margo rose and cleared away the empty bowls and soup tureen, while her mother went to the kitchen and returned with small dishes of fruit.

"I hope everyone likes tinned peaches," Isabel said, her tone half apologetic.

"My favorite," Uncle Sheldon quickly assured her. "It's a wonder you were able to find any, considering the shortage."

She smiled, noticeably relaxing as she and her daughter retook their seats. "Wilfred sometimes takes a jaunt out into the country, where one can find things more easily. The farms and all. Plus we have relatives there."

"Ah, yes. And these peaches are delicious."

"Another spot of tea would make them perfect, my dear," Wilfred hinted. "After all, this is a special occasion, having two lovely girls and an old friend with us to share a meal." He beamed at his daughter before his gaze moved on to include Tricia and her uncle.

"I just started a new pot to brewing," Isabel told him. "It'll be done straightaway."

After the meal ended and the girls had helped Mrs. Wyndham with the dishes, Tricia bid Uncle Sheldon goodbye. Then she and the daughter of the house retired to the bedroom they'd be sharing so Tricia could put her things away.

"I'm so glad we've finally met," Margo confessed, drawing the black drape over the frilly curtains in the floral-wallpapered room before turning on a bedside lamp. She took a seat at a desk positioned in the corner while Tricia unpacked her clothes and stowed them in the closet and an empty drawer in the cherry bureau. "You look exactly like your photograph."

Tricia met her gaze, studying the guileless blond for a moment, admiring the flawless complexion and fine, silky hair, the fragile, delicate features. Then she continued with her task. "Your mother said almost the same thing, the day Uncle Shel introduced us. I wasn't aware that my picture had been bandied about all over Britain."

"It wasn't, Silly. But when Kenny came for supper, he would always talk about his family. He was rather homesick, at times, and missed you all. He was especially proud of you."

Strangely comforted—and saddened—by that news, Tricia closed the dresser drawer on her underthings and sat down on the quilt-covered double bed. "Did· he come here often? I mean, he wasn't one to write home a lot. I know he must have been pretty busy, flying with the RAF. I. . .can't believe he's. . . gone. It's not fair." She made no attempt to suppress the anger and bitterness in her tone.

A sad smile tugged at a corner of Margo's lips. "Fairness and war don't fit together, I'm afraid." She toyed with a fold of her polka-dotted dress. "To answer your question, yes. Kenny came here quite a lot. He was almost part of the family, right from the start. My dad absolutely adored him, and Mum, well, she all but worshiped the very ground he walked on. But. . .if he didn't write home often, then he probably never told your family about me."

"What about you?" Tricia asked, suddenly recognizing a particular glow about the girl she must have been blind not to have seen before.

"Mum wasn't the only one who worshiped the ground your brother walked on," Margo murmured candidly. "He and I were very much in love." Moving a few inches away from the desk, she opened the top drawer and withdrew a framed photograph. Perusing it briefly as her azure eyes misted over, she handed it to Tricia. "I'd never met anyone like Kenny before in my life. He was so dashing, so charming. So very funny."

"That's my brother, all right." Fighting tears herself, Tricia ran a fingertip lightly over his image, one she had never seen, tall and resplendent in his official flight gear, standing beside a battered, camouflaged airplane. "He was voted class clown in school. Our parents were mortified. But he deserved that honor. Nobody in the world could make people around him laugh the way he could." The way he still should be doing, an inner voice insisted.

Margo reached for her hand and clutched it tightly. "Would you mind awfully if we shared some memories of him while I'm here? No one else will let me talk about Kenny. They're so afraid I'll burst into tears or something equally shattering. And I need to talk. I need to say his name out loud, to remember him. Remember us."

"It would probably be hard for both of us. But I would love that." Mustering a smile, Tricia squeezed Margo's fingers.

❧

Doug sagged against the curved frame of the B-17 to regather his wits as the Flying Fortress evened out after its encounter with a swifter, more maneuverable German ME-109 in the skies over northern France. The uninsulated plane could drop bombs with precision from more than twenty thousand feet, and the temperature inside its belly often dropped to minus forty degrees Fahrenheit—or lower—at such high altitudes.

Despite the cold, the scuffle with an enemy fighter had left Doug drenched with perspiration. Smoke from the plane's eleven .50 caliber machine guns left a haze throughout the aircraft's interior. His numb fingers shook as he rewound the exposed film and took it out of his camera. After depositing it into his bag, he put his gloves back on.

The immense plane had looked so huge on the ground in comparison to Hurricanes and Spitfires, the narrow confines inside the thing had come as a shock to Doug. Most of the British crew members were inches shorter than he, yet not even they could stand upright. He especially felt sorry for the gunner in the ball turret, beneath the belly of the plane, who had to remain curled up in a fetal position with his back against the armor-plated door. The two waist gunners, their positions staggered on either side so as not to bump into one another, stood hunched over their machine guns, dressed in steel helmets and goggles. Flak vests topped their one-piece coveralls made of leather padded with fleece. An armor plate contoured to the curve of the fuselage below the windows provided their only protection from enemy flak and bullets.

Left waist gunner Sergeant Marty Hawkes squinted grimly through his goggles as he fingered the tear a nearly-on-the-mark bullet had ripped in his flight suit's sleeve, then shook his head, his relief at not having met his Maker clearly evident in his stance, though his oxygen mask hid his expression.

Doug, noting the man's relief, nodded his own silent appreciation at the fellow's marksmanship in fending off the fighter. Even if the roar of the engine didn't eliminate the possibility of conversation over the bomber's interphone lines, the aircraft commander discouraged unnecessary chatter. That way the channel could be kept open for damage reports or announcements of ME-109s in the vicinity. Doug's ears still rang with the tense interchange that had already occurred during the air battle.

The wiry man returned his attention to scanning the skies for more enemy aircraft.

But the experience was still new to Doug, and he knew it would be some time before he'd forget the sight of the German fighter that had singled them out or the sound of bullets peppering the body of the B-17 like hailstones against a tin roof.

"Another fighter diving from nine o'clock," said someone over the interphone.

"He's in my sights," the right waist gunner said.

Doug glanced outside and ducked just as Sergeant Bram Dunlap took a bead on the enemy plane closing in on them and cut loose a stream of tracers, firing on the target. Overhead, the top-turret gunner's twin .50s pounded away, their reports sounding like cannon shells blowing up inside the bomber. The tail gunner's gun added to the cacophony.

The sky around them blackened with lethal explosions from the deadly accurate German cannon fire from the ground. Equally sobering were the Luftwaffe's fighters that would fly flat out right through the formation, firing long bursts from their guns. Their standard offensive armament also boasted 20 to 30mm automatic cannons whose shells would explode on contact with a solid surface, blowing gaping holes in their unfortunate targets.

Twice Doug had witnessed the horrific sight of a Flying Fortress in the group exploding and spiraling to the earth in flames. Various kinds of debris from the shattered aircraft—emergency hatches, exit doors, prematurely opened parachutes, and assorted plane fragments—breezed by in the slipstream.

His respect for the flyers who flew these missions on a regular basis went up the scale, and he breathed a fervent prayer for the ten-man crews who'd been lost. Perhaps some of the individuals had bailed out; but if so, landing in occupied territory presented a whole new kind of peril. *Look after them, Lord. Keep them safe. Bring them home.*

When the danger was past and the plane returned to a lower altitude nearing England's shores, he removed his oxygen mask and put fresh film into his camera. Then he picked his way past the gunners, who were finally able to relax, to the radio compartment in the midsection of the bomber, where the radio operator monitored all communications. After photographing him, Doug navigated the amazingly narrow catwalk through the now-empty bomb bay to the fore portion of the plane to take a few frames of the pilot and copilot at work.

Hopefully, he'd shot some fairly decent pictures of the crew during the raid and the ensuing air attack, maybe even good enough to aid him in moving up in the ranks. He felt gratified at the memory of the huge columns of smoke the bombing run had left in its wake. But maybe once this crate got back to its base, he'd stay on the ground for awhile.

❧

"So Kendall really enjoyed being a pilot," Tricia mused as she and Margo lay beneath the covers in the pitch blackness of the bedroom after the family had retired.

"Ever so much. He was frightfully good at it, you know," Margo said matter-of-factly. "As if he'd been born with a control stick in his hand. He rose quickly through the ranks to flight leader. Helped, no doubt, by the numerous casualties suffered by the Eagle Squadron in their missions. We lost a number of brave lads among our Yank flyers."

Tricia mulled over the information. "Did he talk about it a lot?"

"No. None of them did, except for the debriefing sessions after a raid. Once those were over, the boys would sort of put the whole affair right out of their minds and go on as though they'd just been off for a day at the soccer matches or whatever."

"But how do you know so much about it, then?" Tricia asked.

Margo gave a soft huff. "Actually, being part of the WAAF, I happened to be based where Kenny was, at North Weald. I was one of the plotters, girls who manned the air-to-ground communication and plotted the action and aircraft positions on the maps."

"So you always knew when Ken was flying."

"Right. I was the one monitoring the transmissions. I–I heard every word he uttered, actually."

"That must have been frightening."

"Quite so. Terribly frightening. Especially. . ."

A peculiar twinge of foreboding slithered through Tricia. "Especially when?"

"That last day. Those. . .final words. He was trying so very hard to make it back to the field. His wingman urged him to bail out, but he felt he could save the plane, bring it back for repairs. He was always trying to save the day, be the hero. And he knew how desperately we needed every fighter. We'd lost so many."

A huge weight of sorrow pressed against Tricia's chest, stealing her ability to breathe. How easily she could picture her brother's valiant struggle in those final moments of his life. But she couldn't begin to imagine what it must have been like for the woman he loved to sit on the sidelines, listening helplessly to her doomed pilot.

" 'Guess I cut things a bit close,' he said," Margo went on, her voice choked with the memory. " 'The gauges are in the red.' Then I heard the engine sputter and cut out. 'I'm goin' in. I'm goin' in. You'll have to fish me out of the channel, Freddie.' " Her words caught on a sob.

Tricia reached for her hand and clutched it hard, not wanting to hear any more, yet needing somehow to know the rest.

"The next was hardest of all to bear," Margo continued, her tone flat. It took a moment before she could muster the resolve to relate it. " 'Are you listening, Margo, Love?' he said. 'I love you, Honey. Tell my parents and Tricia that I love them, too. I'm sorry—' Then the radio went dead. He–he was. . .killed on impact," she choked out.

Weeping openly herself, Tricia couldn't have spoken if her life depended on it. So much anger and outright hatred for Germans seethed inside her. She just held onto Margo's hand for all she was worth as the two of them sobbed into their pillows.

When at last the wave of grief subsided, Margo sniffed and withdrew her fingers from Tricia's grip. "Well, now I've made a jolly mess of us," she said, forcing a lighter tone. "I've got some hankies in my top drawer." Padding across the room in the dark, she returned to the bed with a wad of them. "Be my guest."

"Thanks," Tricia mumbled, accepting the ones Margo held out to her. She mopped her eyes and blew her nose, but any attempt to breathe through her swollen nostrils was futile.

"I'm no longer stationed at North Weald," Margo said calmly, as if giving a weather report. "I just couldn't keep on doing it, listening to other guys on their missions, knowing that some of them would meet the same fate as Kenny. Our headquarters had taken a few hits itself, actually, and one of my closest friends, also a WAAF, was killed. Another was horribly disfigured. I finally requested a transfer to other duties, and now I drive the brass 'round hither and yon, wherever they need to go. And I try very hard not to think about things."

Several silent moments followed. "It's too bad," Tricia finally said.

"What is?"

"Too bad you didn't end up married to my brother. You'd have made a super sister-in-law."

"Ah well, I suppose 'twasn't meant to be."

Tricia pondered the statement. "Do you truly believe some things are destined to be and others are not?"

"I've got to. It keeps me sane. Far better than trying to find some other way to make sense of it, don't you think?"

"I don't know. I really don't know. I want to blame somebody. Hitler, maybe. Or even God. How could He let this happen? Why do there have to be wars? They don't solve anything."

"I suppose because men will always be greedy and want power. Mankind has gone his own way, right or wrong, from the dawn of time. And God allows it because He knows that in the end, He will prevail. Evil men shake their fists in His face and go about doing their worst, but one day He'll bring them to account. Because His will and His purpose always come to pass, no matter how long it takes to do so." She paused. "Only my faith and the peace God has given me inside have kept me going. Helped me deal with my life. . .and my losses."

Not especially liking the turn of conversation to the spiritual side, Tricia didn't answer right away. She couldn't see things quite as simply as Margo did. Kendall's death hurt far too much for her to do that. Doug St. Claire had suggested that in time she might feel differently, that war had a way of changing a person's outlook. But Tricia couldn't see that happening. Not to her.

No matter how many people around her preached at her, she couldn't see how she would ever be that passively accepting.

six

On her first morning in the Wyndham home, Tricia had lain awake for some time when a soft tapping sounded on the bedroom door. She felt the mattress shift as Margo sat up.

"Yes? What is it?"

"Time to dress for services," Isabel said in hushed tones after opening the door a crack. "You two sleepyheads talked half the night. You've barely time to catch a bite before we go."

"Ohh," the willowy blond moaned. "We'll come straightaway."

Tricia yawned and stretched. "Do you think your parents would mind terribly if I begged off? I'm afraid I have a bit of a headache this morning."

"As you wish. I was rather looking forward to having you with us in church, though."

"Yes, so was I," Tricia hedged. "But there'll be other times, I'm sure. I'll close my eyes for a few more minutes, then go out for a walk in the fresh air. That usually helps."

"Whatever you say."

Tricia turned to face the wall and closed her eyes as Margo rose and tiptoed to the closet. But sleeping was the farthest thing from her mind as she listened to the quiet rustle of her friend getting dressed. She truly did have a slight headache, but not one that would have kept her from an activity she desired. Attending church simply didn't fall into that category. And getting out of attending this morning had been easier than she'd dared to hope.

"Is there anything you'd like me to bring you before I go?" Margo asked.

"No, thank you. I'll be fine."

"Well then, I'll see you when we get back. Have a good rest."

For a split second, Tricia's conscience nearly got the better of her, and she considered doing the polite thing and going with her hosts as expected. But she bit down on her lips before saying something she'd regret later. Besides, sitting through a long, tedious, boring sermon would no doubt turn a slight headache into a full-fledged migraine.

Once the stillness of the house indicated that the family had taken their leave, Tricia got up and headed for the bathroom, where she splashed cold water on her face and freshened up. After making the bed and tidying the room, she slipped into a skirt and blouse and went to the homey blue-and-white kitchen, where she found a place set at the table for her. A pot of still-warm coffee and some fresh apple scones waited beside it. With no reason to hurry, she ate slowly, perusing the headlines of yesterday's paper as she chewed. No wonder Britons were weary of this war as it dragged on endlessly.

People back in America needed to be kept abreast of the dreary situation faced by their English cousins. Perhaps her former editor at the Chronicle would accept some first-hand impressions of what was going on over here, get folks actively behind the plight of the average person. She had a whole free day to get busy on an article or two. All she needed was a subject.

After rinsing out the dishes she'd used, Tricia dried her hands and went to the bedroom to retrieve her camera. Muggy air from outside barely stirred the lace curtains on the open windows as she emerged from the house and walked to the nearest bus stop. She had no idea where she'd end up, nor did she particularly care, as long as it was someplace interesting.

❧

Refreshed in his spirit, Doug made his way to the exit of the traditional stone church at the close of the service. The structure didn't resemble his father's white clapboard house of worship back in the States in the least, especially with its damaged pews and patched walls. Some stained-glass windows had been replaced by clear panes. Yet hearing the familiar hymns played and sung ministered to him, and so did the sermon, even though the pastor had read the entire discourse. As usual, the sanctuary had bulged at the seams with somber-faced listeners, each one dressed in somewhat threadbare Sunday best. The war had brought all classes of people together in a way unheard of before the conflict, and friendly smiles and pleasant chatter reigned after the service.

The line of worshipers filed past the white-haired minister as they exited, and when Doug's turn finally came, he clasped the man's veiny hand warmly. "Good sermon, Reverend. Gives a person a lot to think about."

"Myself as well, to be sure," he said, a knowing twinkle in his faded blue eyes. " 'Twas a real pleasure to have you with us again this morning."

"Thank you, Sir." Doug nodded and left for Fleet Street. Taking an entire Sunday off was a luxury none of the team could afford, and he had yet to write the articles that would be cabled across the Atlantic. Reuters News Service would pick up and dispatch whatever photographs the U.S. military had approved from yesterday's bombing mission. Perhaps in the not-too-distant future the newspapers back home would feature an article with his byline. One that made it above the fold. Surely that wasn't too much to ask.

Thinking of the rolls and sheets of film he'd exposed during the flight on the B-17 brought Tricia Madison to mind. It would be hard to resist the temptation to charge into that darkroom this afternoon and develop those shots himself; but after that elaborate speech he'd made on the importance of her presence, he knew the wise thing would be to trust her skills. She'd get to them tomorrow morning.

But how had she fared today? Sheldon Prescott had mentioned his niece would be staying with the Wyndhams, and Doug knew that family to be committed Christians. He could only hope and pray she'd gone to church with them. . .because not even Tricia knew how much she needed the Lord in her life.

❧

Tricia found her venture into the tubes—the subway tunnels

beneath the city—shocking. Narrow and elliptical in shape and stretching as far as the eye could discern in the limited light, the cheerless confines were walled in steel casing. Tracks sliced like a zipper down the middle.

The sight of people, hundreds of them, sitting dejectedly on the hard benches lining either side cinched Tricia's heart. A few appeared to be waiting for the next train. Others had made these tunnels their wartime home, sleeping in their clothes on the benches or on mattresses strewn so closely together on the wooden floor, hardly an inch remained for a person to walk without tripping over someone. They looked old and wretched. Bundled-up and patched-up people whose lined faces indicated they'd experienced precious few of the good things in life were now in a desperate struggle to find any semblance of comfort, however small. Children, too, were there. Seemingly everywhere, the ragged urchins slept soundly or played, laughing and talking in groups, some of them even singing.

Tricia cringed with guilt as people peered up at her when she came along—Miss Fashion Plate America, who had discarded better clothing than the best anyone here sported. She could barely look anyone in the face.

A shabby woman of indeterminate age approached her and eyed her head to toe. Hiding behind the woman's skirts, a stringy-haired little girl in a too-small dress chanced only an occasional peek from the folds clutched in her grubby hands. "Ye lookin' for someone, Miss?"

"I–I'm new in London," she stammered. "With the American press. I was. . .was just. . ."

"Oh, another reporter, eh?" Her watery eyes narrowed with a smirk as they came to rest on Tricia's shiny camera. "Come to find a story to send back to your fine paper."

"I didn't know what I would find," Tricia said in all honesty. "This is my first visit to Britain since I visited my great-grandmother near Birmingham as a child. I can't believe the extent of the horrors that Hitler has put you all through, the devastation he's wrought on this beautiful land."

Perhaps the mention of her own British ties brought about a change, a gentling, of the scornful expression in the older woman; but whatever the reason, Tricia appreciated it immensely. And it helped bolster her own courage.

"Well, he's not done us in," the woman said, straightening her shoulders proudly. "Our brave lads'll get him back good, they will."

"I hope they do." Tricia paused for a breath. "I–I know some of what you feel, though. This war has cost me something, too. My only brother. He flew with the RAF until his plane went down in the channel a few months ago. That's why I've come, really. I can't just stand by and watch our heritage be spoiled by a madman like Hitler. I want to do whatever I can to support the fight that will rid the world of vermin like him."

"Oh, Ducky, that's the spirit." A cackle and a broad smile revealed a missing front tooth. "You're not so uppity as ye looked at first. You're welcome to come visit us any time."

"Thank you." Tricia hesitated, wondering whether the woman would consider her nosy, then went for broke. "May I ask you how long you and your little ones have been living in the tubes?" she queried hopefully, trying not to gawk at the depressing conditions so many unfortunates had been forced to endure as a way of life.

"From day one, I'd say," she replied without emotion. "We'd nowhere else to go, once our house in Chelsea was done in by the bombs. We couldn't even go back for blankets. We had to trust the good Lord to look after us and keep us warm."

Tricia schooled her expression not to register scorn, though it seemed to her that the Lord hadn't gone out of His way to provide for or to keep up the morale of Londoners. She surveyed the ragtag collection of belongings bundled here and there, the baskets of food individuals brought in on a daily basis. Even worse, an old metal bucket for lavatory purposes sat in the middle of the open area as if to flaunt the kind of crude intimacy that had been forced upon the occupants of the shelter. Yet the folks who dwelled under these dreary conditions accepted their fate with incredible cheerfulness as they milled about, visiting with one another, or dozed, oblivious to the constant din of voices and activity around them.

"Would you mind if I took your picture?" she asked suddenly, hardly daring to hope.

The woman frowned in disbelief and planted a fist on her hip. "My picture! What on earth for, Luv? I'm not the beauty I once was before all this happened. Seems to me a pretty Yank like you could find better things to point that fancy camera at than this tired old face o' mine."

"Oh, but your face is ever so interesting," Tricia said sincerely. "It shows strength and courage. . .and trust, as you said a moment ago. I'm collecting pictures of people whose courage I greatly admire."

The dubious expression that added years to her features relaxed a little, and she gave a nod. "Just give me a moment to comb me hair, an' me and my little Ida, here, will pose all nice and proper for ye."

"Thank you," Tricia said, relieved. "Thank you very much."

When at last Tricia returned to the street outside, she had to find a place to sit down for awhile and compose herself. She had believed that Kendall's death had provided her with ample reasons to detest the Third Reich. But this! The senseless suffering it imposed on innocent people with no regard whatever for this beautiful country incensed her even more. She could hardly wait to send America some graphic pictures of the horrors of this war, let them see that the shortages and rationing they were experiencing were worth it, and the brave young men being shipped over here were fighting for a noble cause.

She wandered down many of the city's side streets that day, seeing damage on almost every block. By the time she returned home from her outing, the smell of half the week's meat ration wafting from the Wyndham house announced the supper hour. She hadn't intended to be gone quite so long, and she hoped she hadn't offended her kind hosts.

Margo breezed out to meet her before she got halfway up the front path. "There you are! We were beginning to worry that you'd gotten lost. Or worse."

"I'm sorry. I lost track of time."

"Well, not to worry." She looped an arm through Tricia's and walked with her into the house. "Mum's putting supper on the table. You've come just in time."

Tricia hung the strap of her camera bag on the hall tree as they passed, and they made a quick detour to wash their hands in the kitchen.

The Wyndhams both looked up from their places at the table as the girls entered the dining room.

"Well, hello," Isabel said. "We wondered what had become of you."

"Your headache better by now?" her husband inquired.

"Yes, thanks. I feel much better. The fresh air was just what I needed. So sorry I made you worry." She took the chair they indicated and bowed her head for grace.

After the short prayer, Wilfred peered over his small, round spectacles as he passed the bowl of mashed potatoes her way. "The wife and I want you to know you're quite free to come and go as you please for as long as you're here. But in order to plan meals, we'd appreciate knowing when you won't be here to eat with us."

Feeling more than a little chagrined, Tricia accepted the proffered potatoes and helped herself to a small serving. "Yes, I understand. Please forgive me for being gone so long without word."

"Oh, 'tis quite all right," Margo crooned. "It's no easy thing to get 'round the city these days, what with so many streets in shambles and the others positively clogged with buses and military trucks. It's taken us all awhile to make adjustments. You'll get used to things in no time, wait and see."

The encouraging words helped clear the tension Tricia had felt earlier, and she relaxed.

"You missed a fine sermon at church," Margo's father

announced. " 'Twas just what we needed."

"That's nice," Tricia said absently as his daughter handed her the meat platter. Noting how much china showed around the tiny roast, she took only a thin slice. The garden salad and hot rolls would more than help to fill her up.

"But to make up for your not being able to go," the man declared in all seriousness, "we'll read a double portion of Scripture this evening 'round the table before our customary family prayer time."

Tricia stopped chewing and manufactured a smile. "That's really. . .wonderful."

૨૦

Monday morning arrived long before Tricia was ready for it. And when Margo left bright and early to catch a northbound train to return to her WAAF duties, it was like having to part with a soul mate. The talks the two of them had shared long into the night stayed in Tricia's mind as she rode the bicycle to Fleet Street to start a new workweek. At least she'd made Margo promise to return soon for another visit.

After arriving at the newspaper headquarters, she headed straight for the already half-empty coffeepot. "Good morning," she said, nodding to Dora and Babs as she reached for a clean cup and filled it. She couldn't help noticing the empty desks of their male counterparts.

"How was your weekend, Luv?" Babs asked, a smile broadening her freckled face. "All settled in your new place, are you?"

"Yes, thanks. The Wyndhams seem a wonderful couple. They make me feel welcome and at home, as if I'm part of the family already."

Stylish as always in yet another attractive suit, Dora paused in her typing and glanced up. "I'm billeted with a British family myself, and I've been quite happy with the arrangement. It seems to benefit all of us."

"I feel that way, too." Tricia smiled and carried her coffee to the darkroom, where she found her work basket nearly over-flowing with exposed film waiting to be developed, each group tagged with the names of the individuals who would claim them later. Obviously the news team didn't indulge in the luxury of two-day weekends. Not with a war going on.

Knowing the first order of business was the preparation of fresh chemicals, she gulped down her coffee, then tied an apron over her clothing. As she filled the various baths with the proper mixtures, the familiar distinctive odors blended together and rose to her nostrils. Then she started on the first set of sheet film, anticipating the certain pleasure derived from being the first to see what the men had been up to. Not to be denied, it gave her no little satisfaction to have taken some photos of her own—even without Doug St. Claire to escort her around.

St. Claire. Even his last name sounded religious.

seven

The number of prints and enlargements Tricia had finished by the time lunch hour arrived surprised even her. Easing some kinks out of her shoulders as she swept a critical eye over the display, she removed her work apron and hung it on the hook alongside others. Then she clicked off the NO ENTRY light and opened the door.

Springing to life from his relaxed stance against file cabinets in the hallway, Doug straightened and stepped forward. His dark brows hiked, rippling his forehead. "Oh, good. You're taking a break. Did you happen to do up any of my pictures?"

"And good morning to you, St. Claire," she quipped, deriving a kind of perverse satisfaction when she saw the flush reddening his neck. "As a matter of fact, yes. I've finished nearly everything you turned in. You were pretty busy over the weekend."

"That's true. I was."

She smiled thinly and nodded as she started for the exit in the otherwise-deserted office. Apparently they were the last ones to take advantage of the noon break.

He slid his hands into his trouser pockets and fell into step with her, a slightly cocky grin coming to the fore. "It was my first experience stowing away inside a bomber."

Tricia halted and turned to gape at him. "You stowed away? You mean no one even knew you were aboard?"

"Of course they knew I was there," he said, his grin turning lopsided. "I was being facetious. No civilian gets on a B-17 without going through the necessary procedure. The press has clearance, but it's one of those enter-at-your-own-risk kind of deals."

"Which involves more than just a little risk," Tricia elaborated, reflecting on shots of his she'd developed that portrayed other bombers disintegrating and plunging to earth in smoke. How easily his could have been one of them. She resumed her pace.

So did he. "Yeah, well, as they say, somebody has to do it."

"No doubt."

The abrupt stop this time was his. "What? You think a reporter can get someplace in this world without taking a few chances now and then?"

"Of course not."

"Then what's the problem, Tricia?"

His smoky gray eyes probed her soul, adding sensations she'd never before experienced. Making her more than a little uncomfortable. "I don't have a problem. I was. . .was just. . ." Wondering where the conversation was leading, she released a ragged breath.

"Anyway, it was quite an experience," he said in all candor, "actually being present during a mission, getting to witness what our flight crews face every day, feeling as though I'm part of it. I'm kinda anxious to view my work, know what I mean? See how things turned out."

"You took some great pictures," she admitted, trying her best not to reveal too much of the envy—or was it admiration—inside her.

"I'd sure like to check them out myself, if you don't mind my entering your domain after we grab a bite to eat, that is."

"We?"

"Yeah. Why not? I have to eat. You have to eat. Why shouldn't we have lunch together? There's a nice little coffee shop just a block from here."

For the life of her, Tricia could think of no reason to refuse. "Sure. Why not?"

A short walk on battered sidewalks and alongside damaged buildings took them to a tiny hole-in-the-wall called the Pigeons' Roost. Worn, red-and-white-checked linens lent a touch of faded cheer to an otherwise somber interior crammed with one table too many. Doug ushered her through the maze of chairs, most of which were occupied, to a vacant booth along the side wall. They took seats opposite one another and ordered the specialty, fish and chips. Meanwhile, strains of Vera Lynn's "I'll Be Seeing You" issued from a radio perched on a shelf behind the cash register.

When their food arrived, Doug glanced up at Tricia. "I, uh, usually say grace before I eat. Do you mind?"

"No. Be my guest." But uncomfortable at such displays in public, she didn't close her own eyes. Afterward she munched her portion in near silence, while Doug gulped his down.

He signaled to the waitress for more coffee.

"Will you and your lady be 'avin' dessert?" the hollow-cheeked server asked, glancing from one to the other as she filled both their cups. "We've some fresh peach pie still warm from the oven."

"Sure. Sounds great," he answered for both of them, not bothering to correct her misconception. But he did look across the table at Tricia after the girl had walked away. "Okay with you?"

"Only if you finish the rest of these chips," she answered wryly. "I'm not used to having such a big meal at lunchtime."

"Or any other time?" he teased, flicking an inoffensive-but-appreciative look over her slim frame as he helped himself to the leftovers on her plate.

She suppressed a blush. "I'm not a big eater."

He gave a nod of assent, then sat back while the waitress placed servings of pie before them. "Thanks, Miss." Slicing immediately into his sweet treat, he paused with his fork partway to his lips. "So what made you decide to leave the peaceful home front and plunk yourself in harm's way—if you don't mind my asking?" His mouth closed around the chunk of pie.

"That's easy," she said with a smirk. "I have a score to settle. I knew that being on the front lines of battle with my finger on a trigger wasn't an option, but maybe I could at least be where I could see the Germans get what they deserve." At his confused expression, she added more details. "They killed my brother. He was a pilot with the Eagle Squadron."

Doug's eyes narrowed in thought, then a look of sudden comprehension dawned. "Oh, I get it. Madison. You're Ken's sister. I should've made the connection before."

For a fleeting second, Tricia wondered if her brother's reputation as an ace had made him renowned all over Britain. "You knew Kendall?"

"Not really. I met him once when he came to see Sheldon is all. Your uncle was very proud of his exploits and asked him to come by on his time off so he could work up a feature story to send back to the States. But as things worked out. . ."

Tricia didn't need him to finish. She nodded while toying with her pie.

"I'm. . .sorry. . .for your loss. That would be rough to deal with."

She'd heard the same sentiment dozens of times since Kendall's death. But somehow, knowing that Doug had flown the dangerous skies himself, the simple words rang with true sincerity. Especially when she glanced up and saw the gentleness in his expression. It was nearly her undoing after months of warding off the intense sorrow lurking just outside the gates of her consciousness, months of being strong for her parents. Except for breaking down with Margo that one night, she hadn't really allowed herself to grieve. It was so much easier to focus on the anger instead.

"How long have you been in England?" she finally asked, needing a change of subject.

"Only since the first of the year. I was low man on the totem pole until you arrived, trying to work my way up."

Tricia glanced at her watch, then blotted her lips on her napkin and set it beside her half-empty plate. "Well, then, we'd better not dawdle any longer. You'd best get back out there and cover the news."

"Yes, Ma'am. I fully intend to. . .after I see how those photos turned out."

"Right. I would imagine they've dried by now."

With a hopeful grin, he stood and assisted Tricia. But even as she dug into her purse, he withdrew money from a trouser pocket and placed it on the tabletop. "It's covered."

"Thanks, but I like to pay my own way."

"Next time, maybe. I'm in a hurry." As if to prove his point, he took her elbow and steered her toward the door. Outside, he set a more natural pace as they headed back to the office, threading their way through passersby in uniform. "So how was your weekend? It's the Wyndhams who are putting you up, right?"

"Don't tell me. You know them, too?" Sure is a small world, London, Tricia conceded with a frown.

"Well, you know how it is. Sheldon's a great one for taking his staff places, meeting folks. Especially when they can cook like Isabel Wyndham. It keeps us from missing Mom's apple pie so much."

"Ah. I had a nice weekend, actually. Their daughter came home to visit." Slanting a look up at her lanky companion, Tricia waited for him to name her.

"Hmm. Didn't know they had one. I do know they belong to a pretty good church, though. Did you happen to tag along?"

Tricia gave an exasperated huff. "Are you always this nosy, St. Claire? Or is it just my life you enjoy prying into?"

"Sorry. I was simply making conversation. Scout's honor." He held up his right hand in the traditional Boy Scout pledge.

"And managing to direct it toward religion while you're at it," she muttered. "But to answer your question, no. I did not go to church with them. I went for a walk instead."

"Well, hey. There's nothing wrong with walking."

When he finally lapsed into silence, Tricia sighed with relief.

❧

Bright sunlight blazed down from the midday sky, painting violet and auburn highlights among Tricia's dark waves as Doug walked her back to headquarters. The admiring glances she drew from young men they passed were not lost on him.

Not that he faulted them. Anyone with eyes in his head could recognize class when he saw it. She'd worn tailored slacks and a silk blouse today, yet she appeared utterly feminine from head to toe.

Even now, with that hint of impatience that flattened her rosy lips into a prim line, she carried herself with the calm, quiet assurance of someone who had always been beautiful, but never gave the matter much credence. Her loveliness affected him, though, and made him straighten his shoulders and walk a bit taller.

Mentally he replayed the conversation they'd shared in the restaurant. He could still hear the bitterness in her tone when she made reference to Germans, could still see the glint of outright hatred in her eyes. And though he understood the reasons behind those strong feelings, he knew that, unchecked, they could eat a person alive, chip away at a soul until only a hollow empty shell remained. His own heart ached for her in a way he'd never before experienced. *How do I get through to her, Father? How can I reach her?*

Tricia's voice cut across his prayer. "I never thanked you for lunch. I really did enjoy it. Thank you. Next time it's my treat."

"We'll see," he managed. He'd never yet allowed a woman to pay for his meals and couldn't see himself starting now. Noticing that they'd reached the building housing their offices, he opened the door so Tricia could precede him. Then he followed her downstairs, straight to the darkroom.

"It's safe to go in," she said, grasping the knob and turning it. "I never leave things out that shouldn't be exposed to light."

"Why am I not surprised?" he quipped.

She moved to the area where she'd strung his dried photos. "These shots are yours. I enlarged a few of the best ones and cropped others so more of the details would be clear."

He crossed his arms and went slowly down the line, tapping a fingertip against his lip as he examined each frame in turn. "This is great work!" he finally admitted. "Really great. Now I know why Shel was so insistent on bringing you here."

"You mean you were actually worried?" she asked, genuinely surprised as he made another leisurely trip down the line. "I'm shocked."

He flashed a sheepish grin. "I guess we all have to learn to trust our hard work to the hands of others. I won't doubt you again, that's for sure." His chest puffed out a little just imagining the kudos these shots would garner.

"I'll take that as a compliment."

Reaching the end of his own pictures, he turned to view a few others, fastened to the wire with purple clips. "Whose are these?" He peered closely at the stark features of a tattered woman with a ragged child. The background—obviously an underground shelter—was hazy and indistinct, while the human subjects were exceptionally clear. Taken from several different angles, the composition of each picture graced the pair with an almost tangible dignity despite the ragged clothes and bleak surroundings.

"Uh. . .mine," Tricia said self-consciously. "Just ignore them. I was only fooling around."

He paid her no mind. "This one's Isabel Wyndham, isn't it? Who's the blond? Those are some pretty snazzy poses."

Tricia came to join him. "Their daughter, Margo. Turns out she was my brother's fiancée. She's quite nice. An easy subject."

"She has sad eyes," he said. *Sad, like yours,* he nearly added, but restrained himself.

Tricia turned and walked to her table. "They're just some shots I took over the weekend. Feel free to take yours with you. I really need to get back down to business now."

Doug had the distinct impression she was trying to get rid of him, so he acquiesced. "Think I'll do just that. I need to get these through clearance so I can ship them off with the articles I've been putting together for the Reuters messenger. He'll be picking up our stuff for the Associated Press tomorrow. Thanks. For doing such a good job, I mean."

"Sure. I'll finish the others this afternoon."

"Right." When he'd unclipped the last of his own photos,

he took the stack with him and made his exit. At his desk he went through them a third time, trying to choose which shots he'd have Reuters send off and which ones were better filed away for posterity.

But the longer he looked at them, the less impressed he felt. Sure, they'd been taken in the heat of battle. Sure, they showed action and results, which was most likely what the press expected. But why did they suddenly appear so mediocre?

In disgust he shoved the lot into his top drawer and rolled a clean sheet of paper into his typewriter, then began tapping away with his two index fingers. Even though he'd picked up considerable speed over the years, he still relied on the tried-and-trusted hunt-and-peck method. *And the pictures I take probably aren't much better than my typing, an inner voice accused. Maybe I should relegate myself to permanent darkroom duty. . .and let someone who has a true eye for what makes a photograph memorable take over. Like Tricia Madison.*

eight

Tricia's second foray into the underground shelters, the following weekend, only reinforced her initial findings. Even worse than the first tube, this one crawled with fleas and lice, and mosquitoes flitted about in the fetid air. Cringing in reflex, she hunkered down inside her light jacket and made a quick exit without trying to speak to anyone, much less take a picture.

But she found Aldwych, just off the Strand, to be much more efficiently run. A lavatory system had been installed, and a canteen had moved in to provide meals. The permanent residents still looked weary and forlorn, but good-natured smiles and greetings prevailed as they chatted and milled about. And since she'd arrived just as a train came through to discharge passengers and take others aboard, no one paid much attention to her as she made her way along the makeshift cots lining the walls.

"Will ye be havin' a cup of coffee, Miss?" an auburn-haired young woman with glasses asked as Tricia started past the portable canteen. " 'Tis a bit nippy up top today."

"Yes. Thank you." Accepting the hot drink, Tricia sipped it slowly. "Do you work here every day?"

"Rain or shine, 'tis a fact." She gave a conspiratorial grin. "Keeps me from bein' called up into service, like many of me friends. Shop girls are easy prey, they are."

Tricia had noticed that most of the women tending the stores were middle-aged or older but hadn't given the matter much thought. She observed the slim girl doling out coffee and sandwiches to other passersby.

"I don't mind bein' here, really," the server admitted candidly. " 'Tis better'n most of the tubes. At night we even have entertainment. Actors from the theaters across the way come and perform for the folks, do readin's and the like. Some do numbers from whatever's playin' at the cinema. Gives people a wee treat to look forward to."

"You don't say." Tricia finished her coffee and handed back the cup. "My name is Tricia Madison. And you're—?"

"Lilly Barnes. Lill to my friends. You're a Yank, I see," she added, assessing Tricia's fashionable clothes with no change of expression. "Been in London long?"

"Not really. I'm. . .with the press." A subtle hardening of Lilly's features put Tricia on the defensive. "But that's not why I'm here in Aldwych. I mean, I am working on some feature stories, but not officially. It's more of a personal mission. I'm hoping to rouse more American support. Wake people up to the gravity of the situation here in Britain."

"I see." But despite the flat response, Lilly appeared confused. "Well, no matter. Can't be much need for one more story about us, when there's naught but frightful news on every front of this war nowadays. We'd all just like the whole mess to end so we could get our lives back. What's left of us, that is."

Tricia gave an understanding nod and stood by while Lilly dispensed sandwiches and hot coffee to some new arrivals. "The lady who's billeting me does this kind of work, too," she told the girl after the customers had left. "Perhaps you know her? Isabel Wyndham?"

"Oh, the grand lady herself," Lilly said, arching slender brows. "Before the blitz, none of the uppity types in her circle would deign to give the time o' day to poor workin' lasses like meself. But the bombs fell on them as well as us. Now we're all in the same boat, ye might say."

"Yes. Everyone I've talked to has lost someone or something. A home, a close friend or relative. It's very sad."

Hardly affected by Tricia's statement, Lilly shrugged a shoulder. "So what are ye writin' about?"

"Courage." Tricia smiled. "The faces of courage, to be exact. I've been collecting photographs of interesting people and adding short vignettes of each one. If you have no objections, I'd be honored to take a picture or two of you to add to my project."

Slanting a glance to her left and right, Lilly wrinkled her pug nose. "I'm not in one o' them smart blue-and-scarlet uniforms lots o' me friends are wearin' these days, but if ye don't mind a plain dress, 'tis fine with me."

"Really? Thank you so much! Perhaps we could talk a bit, too." Hardly able to believe her success, Tricia took her camera out of the case and snapped in a fresh flash bulb. The professional side of her had already calculated precisely the aperture and depth of field she'd use to compose these shots to create the proper mood for her spread.

After she finished, Tricia hurried home, determined not to offend her host family again by being late for supper. She hung her jacket and set her camera bag on the step to be taken upstairs on her next trip. Then she went to the kitchen, where Isabel already labored at the sink, peeling potatoes. "May I help?"

"You can chop the carrots, if you like. We're having roast chicken this eve. Wilfred made a trip out to the country and brought us back a fine fat hen. 'Tis all but impossible to buy any sort of fowl at the market these days. But folks who raise them on their farms are glad for a few extra shillings."

"I thought something smelled delicious." Moving to the drain board, Tricia took a paring knife and cut the tops off the garden-fresh carrots, then peeled and cut them into chunks before sliding the pieces into the waiting pot of water. She didn't realize how hungry she was until her stomach reminded her she hadn't eaten since breakfast.

"Did you have a productive day," Isabel asked, "making the rounds of our city again?"

"Yes, as a matter of fact I did. I've met several intriguing people in my travels. I'm hoping to work up a photo essay for my hometown newspaper back in the States."

Her hostess nodded. "I do a bit of writing myself, you know."

"I've noticed you working at the desk some evenings after prayer time. What do you write?"

She opened the oven and removed the lid of the roaster, then spooned some juices over the browning chicken before covering it once again. "I'm one of hundreds of volunteers who send weekly reports to Mass Observation, an organization that likes to keep abreast of things. We jot down our personal thoughts and everyday activities, plus record things that go on around us."

"How fascinating," Tricia mused. She gathered plates, napkins, and utensils for the dining-room table.

"Of course, we're expected to eavesdrop on our neighbors and make note of their feelings, as well as any criticisms they make of government officials; but we've so few neighbors since the bombings. I was rather glad to be relieved of that sort of responsibility. And now with even paper difficult to come by, I wouldn't be surprised if they ask us to cut back to two reports a month."

Tricia reflected on the information. It was hard to imagine someone as forthright as Mrs. Wyndham spying on people. Nor could she think of her as uppity, as Lilly had put it. She seemed so down to earth and unselfish, so concerned for others. A person could do much worse than be as compassionate as Isabel.

"Will you be attending church with us on the morrow, my dear?"

The question, coming so suddenly out of the blue, caught Tricia off guard. "I. . .um. . .will certainly consider it, if I don't oversleep."

"No danger of that, I assure you. I'll rap on your door bright and early."

Tricia manufactured her best smile.

ta

Doug, typing at his desk, heard Tricia arrive and greet the other girls and Paul when she came to work on Monday morning. He caught up with her as she made her way to the darkroom, a cup of coffee in her hand, looking gorgeous in a slim navy skirt and tailored blouse, her side-parted hair dipping into a wave over one ear.

"Morning," he said, remembering his manners this time.

She turned and met his gaze, and the sparkle in those turquoise eyes went straight to his heart. "Good morning. Have a good weekend? Or should I say a productive one?" Her light tone sounded friendly, even sincere.

"Both, actually. I dropped some more film in the basket. No hurry on those, though. It's just some shots of training exercises our boys have been conducting. How was yours?"

"Fine. Thanks for asking. And yes, I went to church." Her lips slid into a smirk as she glanced up at him, then turned the knob on the darkroom.

"Hey, that's great. Glad to hear it."

"Thought you would be. I'd. . .um. . .better get to work now."

"Sure. Gotcha. I have some stuff to do, too. I just wanted to mention my films, that there's no rush and all." Aware that he was babbling like an idiot, Doug shut his mouth as she stepped inside her workroom and closed the door. What was there about the sight of that gal that made his insides go mushy? He shook his head and ran his fingers through his hair, then returned to his desk.

So she'd actually gone to church! *Here's hoping she heard something of benefit. Thank You, Father. Now water those seeds that were planted in her heart. Help her to see her need for You.*

≈

Tricia tied a heavy apron over her clothes and prepared the fresh developing baths so she could get right to work. As always, her baskets brimmed with an assortment of sheet film and exposed rolls to be processed. But she couldn't help smiling at the memory of the expression on Doug's face when she'd mentioned church. Why she'd even bothered to tell him was a mystery. Fact was, she might have been in that scarred sanctuary physically but had tuned out most of the boring sermon with practiced ease. She had far more interesting things to occupy her mind.

One irritating sentence did insist on sticking in her brain, however, like an accidentally swallowed fish bone lodged in a person's throat. *When at last this long trial by fire comes to an end, we must put aside the ill feelings we are harboring inside and forgive those who have wronged us—for then, and only then, can the healing process begin.*

The very concept stung like a slap in the face. *Forgive!* That would be the day. What Tricia wanted to see was every last member of the Third Reich ushered swiftly to his everlasting punishment in the Lake of Fire, assuming it existed. And in their case, she hoped it did.

As always, she processed the men's work before starting on her own; and today there was so much of theirs, she knew her pictures would have to wait a day. But there was no rush on those anyway. She'd wired a query to her former editor back at the *Chronicle* to see if he'd be interested in a photo spread or feature articles. Until she heard from him, she'd just continue compiling photos and writing the vignettes as spare time permitted.

When the noon break arrived, dark-haired Ned Payne loitered in the hall outside the darkroom, a typically flirtatious glint in his blue eyes. "Hi, Doll," he said, inching a little too close and draping an arm around her shoulder. "Hope you're done with the shots I took."

Tricia filled her lungs slowly for patience as she hiked her brows and shrugged out from beneath his grasp. "Don't," she said icily. "Don't do that."

He had the grace to look abashed. "Sorry. I didn't mean anything by it. Just being friendly."

"I prefer my friends to act like gentlemen."

"Right. I'll try to remember that." He hesitated a few seconds, then picked up the original subject as though there'd never been an interruption. "Well, did you finish my pictures?"

"Yes, I did them. They're drying now. You can go in and look them over, if you like."

"Thanks. Will do. And. . . ." He cleared his throat. "Please accept my apologies. I forgot you're not used to me." A stupid grin quirked his thin lips, and he opened the darkroom door and went in.

Across the office, Dora and Babs snickered.

"He's a fine one, isn't he, our Ned?" Babs said, rolling her eyes. "Always sees himself as irresistible to the fair sex. Thank goodness Paul is more subtle when he flirts—which isn't often, since he's so rarely here to be a bother."

"I suppose Ned's harmless enough," Tricia ventured.

"Especially when put in his place, as you did so handily," Dora added. "We were just about to go out for a bite. Care to join us?"

"I'd love to." She waited for the pair to grab their purses and jackets; then the three of them grabbed their umbrellas and headed out into the rainy day.

The sight of the Pigeon's Roost brought Doug St. Claire to mind. Half-expecting to see him in the small restaurant, Tricia swept a glance around the busy room while shaking raindrops from her umbrella and parking it in the stand with the others. But he was not among the patrons.

"They serve the most wonderful pasties here," Babs said, her freckled face bright with a smile as they seated themselves at an unoccupied table.

"Meat and potato pies," Dora explained, "in case you're not familiar with the term. I've grown rather fond of them myself. Mrs. Sheffield, my landlady, often makes them." She paused. "It's also one of her son Ronald's favorite dishes."

After they placed their orders and the food arrived, the girls settled down to eat. Tricia hesitated before digging in, just in case either of her companions was inclined to say grace, the way Doug had. She was a tiny bit disappointed when they didn't.

"Seems you mention Ronnie quite a bit of late," Babs teased as she cut into her slice of meat pie. "Is there something serious going on?"

A faint blush tinted Dora's high cheekbones. "Well, a girl

can get pretty tired, waiting for that confirmed bachelor St. Claire to notice her. Ronald's been taking me out whenever he's home on leave. He's quite. . .nice. I wouldn't be at all surprised if something serious was in the making. Besides, I've always been a little enchanted by British men, with their always-so-proper accents and all."

"Well, praise be!" Babs said, tracing celebratory circles in the air with her fork. "Except for the accent part. I've never noticed one. . . ."

But Tricia was still concentrating on the statement about Doug's being a confirmed bachelor. Not that she minded, exactly. He just didn't come across to her that way. Regardless, it would take a certain type of woman to make him sit up and take notice, for sure. She'd have to be extremely religious. . .be on an inside track with the Divine Being.

"And how do you like pasties, Tricia?" redheaded Babs said, breaking into her thoughts. "Aren't they just magnificent?"

At that moment, the man himself strolled into the restaurant. His eyes met Tricia's across the crowded space, and his almost imperceptible wink made her heart do a peculiar little flip-flop. "Yes. Magnificent. That's just the word that comes to mind."

"Ladies," Doug said with a nod as he passed by, his gaze lingering a few seconds on Tricia. He took a seat at an adjacent table.

Even when the waitress blocked her view of Doug, Tricia was immensely aware of his presence. . .and of how much she'd have preferred to be listening to him talk than Dora and Babs.

This was not good. Not good at all.

nine

September 3 marked the beginning of the fourth year of the war in England. In recognition of the grave anniversary, the people of Britain purchased Union Jacks and assembled at 11:00 A.M. to hear the special broadcast from Westminster Abbey before returning to their daily grind.

Later that evening, in the Wyndhams' comfortable parlor, the family gathered to listen to Prime Minister Churchill's nightly speech over the radio. Tricia watched her hosts' expressions turn from grim to downright despondent as their leader droned on about the latest somber news regarding the war.

She'd overheard enough talk between Londoners in her travels to realize folks considered this summer and autumn of 1942 to be the dreariest time since the beginning of the conflict. The news had been bad since spring. Singapore had fallen, and then Burma and Java. The U.S. troops on the Bataan Peninsula surrendered, Germany appeared to be heading for victory in Africa and Russia, and shipping losses in the Pacific were staggering. The victories that once cheered everyone up had petered out, and there wasn't even a bombing raid to spur them into the defense of their city. The neighborliness spawned by shared misery also waned, and people began to resent the American servicemen for their better living conditions, leisure time, and abundance of ready cash.

England's masses weren't exactly starving, but rationing had reduced the national diet to a dull, starchy minimum that sapped energy and left them pasty-faced and susceptible to illness. Folks were forever yawning and tired; and coughs, colds, and stomach troubles prevailed.

"I don't know how many more times I'll be able to patch

this tweed jacket," Isabel said dolefully as she peered over her sewing glasses at her husband. "You've quite worn the elbows through. Perhaps you shouldn't have given away so many of your best suits."

He blew out a weary breath. "What else is one to do when so many of our countrymen are in dire need? And I've not passed along half as much of my attire as you have of yours, my dear. Just do your best. Things must last till war's end. Not many of us can enjoy the sort of warm, sturdy clothing and shoes the Yanks are strutting about in."

As if suddenly conscious of his thoughtless remark, he blanched. "Oh. I beg your pardon, Tricia. I wasn't referring to you."

She smiled. "I know you weren't. I wasn't offended in the least. Even I have noticed how the daily newspapers report on all the money my countrymen are flinging around, hiring taxis, filling your restaurants and movie houses to overflowing. I'm embarrassed that Americans seem so insensitive to England's plight."

"What bothers me," Isabel chimed in, "are all the silk stockings and chocolates they lavish upon poor shop girls who've been deprived of such luxuries far too long. There's no way our own boys can compete with that, even if they were still around to protect their interests, which of course, they are not. And the dreadful conduct of our young women! Parading about Piccadilly Circus and Rainbow Corner like painted hussies. Getting themselves in the family way just so they won't be called up. It's quite the disgrace. Tsk. Tsk." She shook her neatly groomed head. "What will be left of our dear Britain when all this horrid business ends?"

No one responded. When Churchill's address concluded and a program of popular music took its place, Wilfred got up and put on a sweater from the closet. " 'Tis a bit chilly this eve and likely to get worse between now and spring. They say coal's in even shorter supply than it was last winter. Anyone else need a wrap?"

Isabel declined and continued sewing.

"No, thank you," Tricia answered. "But I will put on some coffee for us all. That might help a little." While she waited for the pot to finish perking, she tidied up a few odds and ends that remained from supper. Then she poured three cups of the fresh brew and carried them into the parlor on a tray.

The trill of the doorbell filled the house.

Isabel stopped sewing and glanced up while her husband answered the summons.

"I believe you have a visitor," he announced to Tricia, returning with the caller right behind him.

"Me?" she asked, handing her hostess a china cup. She raised her lashes and saw Doug's tall form, his tawny head nearly touching the top of the archway.

"Mrs. Wyndham, Tricia," he said with a gracious nod toward each of them. Then he centered his attention on Tricia as he toyed with the hat he held in his hands.

A jolt of warmth went through her. "Why, hello. What brings you out here in the dark of night?"

He grinned. "A big package came for you after you left the office. Your uncle thought it might be something you needed and were waiting for, but he was tied up, so I offered to bring it. I bummed a ride on a truck heading this way."

"A truck! How big is the package, for pity's sake? It must be from my parents. Who else would be sending me anything?"

"Come see for yourself," he said. "I left it out in the hall, right beside the door."

Feeling as excited as a little girl on her birthday, Tricia nearly spilled Mr. Wyndham's coffee in his lap as she hastily served him before chasing after Doug.

"From my parents. I just knew it," she proclaimed a moment later, checking the return address of the large cardboard box waiting for her.

"Need help opening it?" Doug asked, producing a pocketknife from his jacket. "Or would you prefer I lug the thing to your room so you can have privacy?"

"Forget privacy. Looks like the censors have already rifled through it. Slice away." She stepped aside to give him room to work; and after a few quick cuts along the rows of tape and the knotted cord strapping the carton, he yanked the flaps open for her.

Tricia knelt to peer inside, then gasped in amazement. "Oh! Look at all this stuff! I needed some of these toiletries." She began taking out a series of smaller boxes one by one, each wrapped in brown paper and cushioned with new linen kitchen towels—another item in short supply since the war.

"Tea," she exclaimed. "Would you believe it? The stuff's rare as gold here these days. And chocolate. And sugar. And even a smoked ham. There's definitely gonna be a celebration at the Wyndham house—and you, my handsome hero-of-a-delivery-man, are invited!" Then, realizing what she'd blurted out without a second's hesitation, she felt heat flood her cheeks. "I mean, if you'd like to celebrate with us, that is. Whenever we have our little feast."

"Hey, I've never been one to turn down a good meal, you know," he teased with his most charming grin. "I'd be happy to oblige."

Still a touch flustered, Tricia folded her arms, trying to collect herself, and nodded. "Good. Good. I'll let you know when to come. In the meantime, there's fresh coffee, if you'd care for some."

"Don't mind if I do," he said. "It's getting kinda cold outside now that fall's here."

She led the way back into the parlor. "Please, have a seat. I'll be right back."

&

Vaguely acquainted with the Wyndhams, but not enough to feel at ease in their home, Doug sat stiffly in the overstuffed parlor chair after each of them had extended the usual polite pleasantries. Idly he tapped an index finger on his knee. He smiled at Isabel when she glanced his way, then at Wilfred, while the old mantel clock ticked, ticked, ticked away the silence. He wished they'd have left the radio playing.

Finally, Tricia returned with his steaming coffee, and the atmosphere of the whole room brightened.

"You'll never guess what my parents have sent us," she told her hosts. "Tomorrow morning you'll have tea with your breakfast, tea with dinner, and again in the afternoon and at suppertime, if you wish. And there's sugar for baking scones or whatever else you desire. Best of all, they included a ham."

"Praise be!" Isabel murmured. "God is so good."

"Yes. Rather," her husband agreed. "He does provide for His own."

To Doug's amazement, the sentiments hardly fazed Tricia. She just kept beaming from ear to ear. He had yet to recover from the stunning vision she'd made when examining the treasures, her blue-green eyes glowing, a tremulous smile on her lips. At the office she was efficient and professional and in control; but here, in this home, dressed in casual slacks and knitted house slippers, she revealed a different side. Soft. Incredibly soft. Vulnerable. Fragile. And desirable. And off limits to a committed Christian like himself.

Some of the brilliance of the moment dimmed. He took a gulp of coffee.

"So I hope you don't mind," he heard Tricia say. "I've invited Doug to share the meal with us."

"Not at all, my dear," Mrs. Wyndham said. "This is your home as long as you're in London. Your friends are always welcome here."

"Thank you," she breathed and stooped to plant a kiss on the finely lined cheek. "I do appreciate the way you've both made me feel at home here."

"We shall enjoy that ham on Sunday, after services. And you are quite welcome to come to church with us as well," Isabel added, directing her gaze to Doug.

"I'd be happy to," he replied. But he'd caught the tiny frown of distaste that crossed Tricia's expression at the mention of church. It made him all the more determined to keep praying for her.

"Well," he said, rising. "I'd better hoof it back to the hotel before it gets much darker. I do thank you for the coffee."

"You're quite welcome," Mrs. Wyndham said.

"I'll see you to the door," Tricia offered, preceding him. She stopped when they reached the exit. "Thanks so much for coming all this way just to bring me that box from home, Doug. It made my evening."

He could hardly draw breath at the glorious light in those eyes of hers. "Anytime. Nothing's too good for a. . .friend." The term didn't quite fit. He'd have liked to use one representative of a relationship slightly closer than that, only he had no right to do so. Besides, she'd given no real indication that his attentions were welcome.

"I've so wanted to do something special for the Wyndhams," she added without missing a beat. "They're such dears."

He knew he'd been out of line harboring hope that he and Tricia might someday grow beyond friendship. But when her words gave no hint of such an inclination on her part, Doug's spirit crashed and burned. "Right. I'll. . .uh. . .see you day after tomorrow, then."

"Right. Sunday." She gave a wry smile. "Beats all, doesn't it? How they always manage to keep me going to church."

They're not the only ones, he almost said, but she never gave him the chance as she quickly added, "Oh well, maybe it'll do me some good, right?"

He stared at her for a timeless moment but kept his answer light. "It couldn't hurt."

≈

Tricia pulled the covers all the way up to her ears and snuggled into the warm comfort of her bed. What a wonderful surprise, the package from home. She'd written several letters to her parents since her arrival in Britain, newsy missives about people she'd met, places she'd visited, and some of the hardships everyone faced because of the war. But she'd never asked them to ship anything her way. Now that a package had come, though, she'd thank them profusely, especially since they'd enclosed a note saying others would follow for Thanksgiving and Christmas. The Wyndhams deserved some return on their unselfishness, even if they did equate them as blessings from God. She smiled to herself.

Then thoughts of the messenger surfaced. How embarrassing to have called Doug her handsome hero-of-a-deliveryman. Hopefully he hadn't caught that slip of the tongue. Of course he was devastatingly handsome, she admitted. Nobody could deny that. Maybe as devastatingly handsome as the hero of a romance novel, even. But to have actually said that! Her face burned with humiliation.

Still, it had been so nice of him to come by unexpectedly the way he had. His presence somehow filled the parlor, leaving scarcely air enough for anyone else to breathe. It seemed the more she got to know him, the more things about him she appreciated. He was pleasant to work with, easy to talk to over a meal, and now she'd discover how he conducted himself at church. No doubt he'd feel right at home there, being on intimate terms with the Almighty. As far as she could see, that was his only fault.

Why, oh why, did he have to be so religious? If not for that, he'd be. . .perfect. Stifling a sigh, she turned over and closed her eyes.

≈

A chilly wind filled with moisture from the Thames made Doug's walk back to his room at the Savoy Hotel less than ideal. And by the time he got there, wisps of fog drifted beneath the slitted red and green of the traffic lights. Approaching the main entrance, he turned down the collar of his bomber jacket and went inside, struck, as always, by the brilliance of the lobby as he passed through on his way to his room. Such a contrast from the blackout darkness of the city.

It was getting harder and harder to keep thoughts of Tricia Madison from dominating his every waking moment.

Something about her struck a chord inside him that had been silent until she had given it voice. Yet she held such disdain for his faith, and the Lord was the most important person in his life. No one had to remind him about God's warnings against unequal yokes. He'd committed that particular passage to memory as a youth.

Of course, he'd been too busy with church activities with his dad, then with college studies after that, to even consider forming a lasting relationship with a member of the fair sex. Besides, with a war going on now, it was folly for anyone to become too attached to someone else. And he was still young, not even pressing thirty yet. Still, what was there about Tricia that tugged so at his heart?

Shucking his clothes, he pulled pajama bottoms on, then turned down the bedspread. But before climbing in between the cool sheets, he slipped to his knees. He didn't know exactly what to pray for Tricia, but he could at least lift her up before the Lord and ask Him to work in her life. Ask Him to prepare her heart for Sunday so that whatever the sermon was about, it might awaken something within her that would eventually draw her to the Lord.

And help me, Father, not to do or say anything that would cause her to lose respect for me or to hinder her from turning to You.

Hoping that was sufficient, he crawled into bed. But sleep was the farthest thing from his mind.

ten

Doing her best not to fidget through the interminable Sunday service, Tricia shifted uncomfortably on the hard church pew. On her right, Isabel smiled at some statement made by the minister that Tricia didn't even understand. And on her left, utterly gorgeous in a charcoal pinstripe suit, Doug jotted notes regarding the passage on a sheet of paper tucked inside the frayed cover of his Bible.

For the life of her, Tricia couldn't see what her companions found so wonderfully fascinating about the preacher's seemingly unending recitation, a continuation of the previous week's sermon on forgiveness. Obviously the man had a one-track mind.

As he droned on, she allowed her gaze to meander over the assortment of dismal hats perched on the heads of women seated in the rows ahead and the balding spots of the men beside them. Floating dust motes caught in a ray of sunlight streaming through the window drew her attention next, and in the minuscule patch of sky visible from her vantage point, she spied a bird soaring on a current of wind. She coveted such freedom.

As she released an unbidden sigh, the minister's voice penetrated her consciousness.

"Last week we studied the conditions of forgiveness and the conduct of forgiveness," he said. "Today we've looked at aspects concerning an unforgiving spirit. But before we close, I'd like us to look at the consequences of not forgiving others. Consider the words of Jesus recorded in Matthew, chapter six, verses fourteen and fifteen."

Tricia felt a gentle pressure on her left side as Doug moved his Bible toward her, his index finger indicating the appropriate place in the chapter. She dutifully looked down and followed along.

" 'For if ye forgive men their trespasses, your heavenly Father will also forgive you: But if ye forgive not men their trespasses, neither will your Father forgive your trespasses.' "

Tricia stared hard at the words.

"Our great nation has suffered immensely during the past few years," the pastor continued, "and will likely go on suffering until complete victory comes to one side or the other. But as that end draws nearer, we must turn our efforts to life. Let us not give in to hatred and anger. God has promised that vengeance belongs to Him. Let us bear in mind that the degree of forgiveness each of us will find for the wrongs we have done to others will ultimately depend upon the degree of forgiveness that we, in turn, have extended to others. May our hearts find no room for unforgiveness, no hindrance to the sweet fellowship we share with Almighty God." He paused, looking out across the solemn congregation. "Now, let us pray."

As all heads bowed and all eyes closed, Tricia swallowed a lump of incredulity. Did these people actually believe what had just been spoken from the pulpit? She had never murdered anyone or stolen anything. She tried to treat people with kindness. What did she need forgiveness for? The whole theory was ludicrous.

But apparently her companions didn't share her sentiment. After the benediction had been pronounced, they stood and exchanged pleasantries with those around them, commenting on the "wonderful sermon" as if the minister had spoken their very minds.

"Nice little church they have," Doug commented, tucking his Bible under his arm. "There's a sweet spirit here, don't you think?"

Tricia turned and gazed up at him. "I, um, never thought about it. I suppose the people are all friendly enough." She followed the Wyndhams out of the pew and to the exit, where they shook hands with the minister. But she was so preoccupied with the skirmish going on in her head, she barely paid attention as her landlords introduced Doug to the man robed in black.

"I would imagine that lovely ham is warmed through by now," Isabel remarked on the short walk back to the house. "It shouldn't take any time at all before we can sit down to a lovely meal."

Wilfred snorted. "I'm afraid my stomach nearly embarrassed the lot of us, merely anticipating it. 'Twas most fortunate that the organ played at just the right time."

"I can relate to that," Doug piped in, and a collective chuckle passed among them.

Delicious aromas greeted them as they entered the front door. Isabel and Tricia hurried to the kitchen and tied ruffled aprons over their Sunday dresses. Then the two of them bustled about, preparing vegetables, mashing potatoes, and making gravy from the rich ham drippings. They'd left the dining-room table set in readiness, so once the bowls and platters of hot food were carried in and set in place, Isabel summoned the men.

While Wilfred seated his wife, Doug pulled out a chair for Tricia, then took the one opposite her. "Mm. Everything sure smells good."

"Perhaps you would like to do the honors," the man of the house suggested and bowed his head.

"Our precious Father," Doug began, "how thankful we are for Thy wondrous goodness to us. We ask Thy blessing on this incredible bounty and upon the unselfish hearts of those who sent it. Bless it to our use, and help us to serve Thee always. And may Thy mercy rest upon this household. In Jesus' name, amen."

As the soft amens echoed Doug's words, Tricia spread her napkin over her lap. But a curious warmth flowed through her at the thought of him praying a special blessing for her parents.

"After you," he said, offering the potatoes to her as the other steaming foods began their way around the table.

"Such a lovely day," Isabel commented, a wistful smile lighting her blue eyes. "And such a treat. I shall never forget this. I must write your mother and father immediately after we eat and express our heartfelt appreciation for their kind generosity." She ate slowly, savoring each mouthful.

Tricia had to smile, though, when Wilfred helped himself to seconds—something she had never before seen him do. The mere thought of how long they'd been deprived of things they once had probably taken for granted made her eyes mist over.

"Well, I have to tell you," Doug said, forking another slice of ham onto his plate, "everything tastes as good as it looks. I'm sure glad you invited me."

"How could we not?" Isabel asked, arching her brows. "It's much nicer to share a blessing with friends. I'm sure our Tricia appreciates having another young person around to visit with after enduring our endless prattle."

"But I love hearing you both talk," Tricia quickly assured her. "The accounts of your experiences are so fascinating."

"Nevertheless," the older woman countered with a warm smile, "I shan't expect you to waste any of this wonderful day cleaning up once we've finished. You two youngsters should go for a walk, do something special. After all, you've very little time to simply enjoy yourselves during the workweek."

The thought hadn't entered Tricia's mind, but now that Isabel mentioned it, the idea blossomed. There'd been so many rainy days lately, she hadn't had many opportunities to get out her camera and seek out willing or interesting subjects.

Doug grinned at Tricia. "Sounds great. What do you say we mosey over to Hyde Park and watch some baseball?"

"Baseball," Wilfred chided with a good-natured snicker. "Hardly more than glorified rounders, if you ask me."

"Maybe," Doug said. "But whatever it is, us Yanks like it. And we play it well."

"Humbly speaking, of course," Tricia couldn't help adding with a light laugh.

Doug shrugged, unconcerned. "Well, all I know is the

Sunday games are drawing quite a crowd every week. So somebody must enjoy it."

"If you're ever going to be on your way," Isabel chimed in, "methinks we'd best serve the chocolate cake Tricia baked." She stood and picked up the leftovers.

"A ham dinner and chocolate cake, too?" Doug said, pretending to swoon. "I may never want to leave."

"Men," Tricia teased, rising to help clear the table. "All they ever think about is their stomachs."

"I beg to differ," he countered, eyeing her with a look that made her blush. "Occasionally we do have other things on our minds."

Before she speculated too deeply about that remark, Tricia grabbed as much as she could carry and beat a hasty retreat to the kitchen to join their hostess. Then, after fanning her scalded cheeks, she put on a gracious air and swept back into the dining room, bearing slices of her masterpiece. She served the men first, then returned for hers and Isabel's servings, while the older woman brought in a fresh pot of tea.

Afterward, Tricia and Doug strolled to Hyde Park in companionable silence. Deciding her softly draped jersey dress wasn't too fancy for the occasion, Tricia stayed in her church clothes. At her side, Doug loosened his tie and removed his suit jacket, which he hooked on one finger and slung over his shoulder in the mild September day.

A gentle breeze stirred the treetops and nudged puffy clouds across the cerulean sky. But the quietness ended once they neared the open area where the boisterous game—which appeared to be army versus a combination of navy personnel and marines—took place.

"Hey, Doug. Tricia," Paul Reynolds called, coming from the sidelines to join them, a speculative expression on his face. "What are you two up to?"

"Nothin' much," Doug quipped. "Just church and dinner. Now we're checking out the game. What's the score?"

"Navy just tied it up. It's the bottom of the fourth." Glancing back toward the action as he spoke, his cobalt eyes glinted. "Guess I'll see you guys around," he said and sauntered in the direction of a cluster of brightly dressed young women who had just arrived.

"Well, we might as well be comfortable." Doug shook out his suit jacket and spread it on the grass, then gestured for Tricia to be seated.

"You're kidding, right?"

"Nope, not at all. Go on. You can't hurt it."

"If you're sure. . ." Shoving aside her misgivings, Tricia dropped down, folded her legs, and demurely arranged her skirt over them.

When Doug occupied the spot right beside her, his long legs stretched out in front of him, she faced a real challenge: how to concentrate on the game, when the breeze swirled the spicy scent of his aftershave around her nostrils.

"Say," he said out of the blue. "Let me have your camera, will you?"

"Whatever for?"

"Just thought I'd take a picture of you in Hyde Park so you could send it to your folks."

Tricia opened the case she'd toted along and handed him her Exacta. She felt a touch conspicuous, turning this way and that while he directed her moves and snapped photos. But at least she found consolation in knowing she'd be the one to develop them, in case she ended up looking as ill at ease as she felt.

Then, when she least expected it, Doug flagged down an unsuspecting passerby and asked him to take a couple frames of the two of them together. Just then a playful gust of wind tossed a tendril of Tricia's hair over one eye, and Doug brushed it away with the backs of his fingers, sending quivery sensations spiraling to her toes. "Say cheese," he whispered nonchalantly into her ear as he moved in close for a final shot or two.

Tricia couldn't help herself. She crossed her eyes and made a face instead. It was easier to clown around than to analyze the strange new yearnings being away from the office with Doug aroused within her.

❧

It was Tricia's perfumed hair that really got to him. Doug had caught the tantalizing scent of it on the walk to church. And every time she moved during the service, the floral essence drifted his way. About the only time he didn't notice it was during dinner, when the stronger smells of food overpowered the more subtle fragrance. But here it was again, under his nose as the two of them waited for that stranger to take their picture and the wind tickled his face with some soft, silky strands. He slowly filled his lungs with her perfume as he brushed her hair away from her eyes, then he filled his gaze with the vision she made in a classy teal dress that matched those glorious eyes perfectly.

Remember, she's off limits, his conscience reminded him.

He cleared his throat and stood. "Let's go find something a little more interesting to finish up the roll, okay?"

"Sure. I'm game." She favored him with a smile and accepted his proffered hand to help her up. Then the two of them left the loud confusion of the baseball game behind.

Hyde Park, once a favorite deer hunting ground of Henry VIII, was in its glory. Together with the adjoining Kensington Gardens, it appeared like an emerald jewel that sparkled from any angle. Velvety lawns interspersed with ponds, flowerbeds, and sedate trees drew war-weary people away from the dreary scars of bombed buildings and ruined streets. Though it had taken a few hits itself, nature, aided by the efforts of dedicated townspeople, had quickly repaired the damage and restored the refreshing beauty that spoke to one's soul.

"Oh! Look at those boats," Tricia exclaimed, spotting some hardy individuals rowing long, slim crafts on the forty-one-acre lake known as the Serpentine. "I'd like a picture of them." She focused her camera and snapped away.

"Tired of walking?" Doug asked after they'd strolled partway around the sapphire blue water.

"A bit."

He spread out his jacket again, and she sank down onto it with a grateful smile.

"It's going to be hard to get back to the grind again tomorrow morning after this wonderful day," she breathed.

"Sure is. I don't usually take the whole day off. Seems there's always something I need to be covering."

Tricia turned and met his gaze. "Do you think this war will ever really be over? Will life ever get back to normal for these poor, unfortunate people?"

"I hope so. We're doing about as much as we can now. Our troops always seem to be busy conducting practice maneuvers, so the powers that be must have something in mind. Hitler doesn't have unlimited manpower or resources, particularly in view of the fact he's spread his forces out thin to attack multiple fronts. And the bombs our side's been dropping on German airplane factories and munitions plants have hurt their cause. I don't think the war can go on indefinitely."

Tricia mulled over his words while studying her nails. "I just feel so bad for folks like the Wyndhams, who've given and given and given so much of themselves and their personal reserves to help people in need and now must do without themselves. I want to help them, make their lives easier."

Doug smiled. "I think you're already doing that, just being there for them, adding your ration points to theirs, making them less lonely for their daughter."

"Ah yes. Margo. I hope she comes for another visit soon. Maybe for Thanksgiving. That would be so nice. She's religious, too, you know. But she doesn't rub it in."

"Do I?"

She met his gaze straight on. "I don't know. Not in anything you say. But sometimes I wonder how you can be so. . . cheerful all the time."

"What can I say? I'm just a happy guy."

She smirked.

"Aren't you happy, Tricia?"

Her head drooped slightly, and she shrugged. "I'm beginning to wonder what happiness is. Seeing all the suffering around me, hearing nothing but bad news day after day, knowing that the beasts who murdered my brother are killing other people's brothers and sons and fathers. . . How can a person be happy about that?"

"I guess it comes from within, from the peace we have inside. No one can be happy about those things, but we can rejoice despite them."

"There you go, getting preachy on me. Who in the world uses words like rejoice?"

Doug searched her eyes, and seeing that she wasn't really offended, only confused, took heart. "Hey, I was just answering your question. I know this country's a mess right now. I know that even though the Germans aren't dropping bombs on us at the moment, that doesn't mean they won't start back up as soon as they get the chance. We're all in danger. We could get killed as easily as any foot soldier on the front lines. But I have no reason to fear death."

" 'Cause you forgive your enemies, like the preacher says?"

He smiled. "More like 'cause I've been forgiven myself."

"Of what? You're nothing like those rotten fiends in the Third Reich. You don't go around killing innocent people for the thrill of conquest. Why should you need forgiveness?"

"Because none of us is perfect. And perfection is the standard God demands."

Tricia only stared at him, a frown causing her slender brows to dip toward her nose. "Now I really don't understand."

"It's not that complicated. There's Someone who did live a perfect life on earth. God's Son, Jesus. And He bought God's forgiveness for our sins with His blood, when He died on the cross. When we admit we cannot measure up on our own and we accept the salvation He provided, He fills our hearts with peace. Then we don't need to fear death. We know we'll spend eternity with Him."

"You really believe that, don't you?" she asked, obviously still puzzled.

"Absolutely. Enough to bet the ranch on it."

She let out a ragged breath. "Well, it's all very interesting, I'll say that. I'll have to think about it for awhile."

"Tell you what," he said. "I always carry a few gospel tracts in my jacket pocket. I'll leave you one. Then you can read it whenever you like. I'm sure the Wyndhams have a Bible they'd let you use, if you'd care to look up the verses quoted in the tract."

Tricia shook her head back and forth. "I'm not making any promises. . . ."

"I'm not asking you to. I'm just trying to help out a friend. Isn't that what you'd do?"

She smiled. "At least you're not pushy, St. Claire. I really thought you would be."

"Then I'm glad I disappointed you, I guess. Come on. I'll walk you home." He offered a hand, and she placed her fingers in it, her slight weight feather-light as he helped her to her feet. Doug didn't know if he'd made any progress in getting through to Tricia. But her questions proved that she was at least thinking about things. Somehow that knowledge provided a ray of hope. He'd keep on praying for her and leave the matter in God's hands.

eleven

Tricia had a lot to think about as she started a new workweek. In the solitude of her bedroom she'd read several times through the religious pamphlet Doug had given her, but she couldn't completely accept its premise. How could there be only one way to God? And as always, the sermons on forgiveness she'd heard at the Wyndhams' church nagged at her like a toothache. But she had to admit she envied the peace her coworker and her host family displayed despite their circumstances; and even though she couldn't understand it, part of her yearned for even a tiny slice of that calm serenity.

Preparing the new batches of chemicals the job required, she heard a knock on the darkroom door and crossed to answer it. "Uncle Shel!" At the sight of his big, crinkle-eyed grin, she leaned out to hug his burly frame. He had on khaki clothing again, a sign that he'd be out of the office and in the field.

"Hi, Snooks. You didn't have the NO ENTRY light on, so I took a chance it was okay to drop off some more film."

"It sure is." Tricia held out her hands, and he filled them with sheet film. "Where've you been? Seems I haven't seen you for ages."

"Let's see." He rubbed his chin. "Everywhere, pretty much. I checked out our newest military installations, interviewed the company commanders, and photographed a bunch of practice maneuvers being conducted."

"But at least you were in Britain the whole time. So you've been relatively safe."

"So far, yes. What've you been up to? All the guys treating you okay?"

She nodded. "Everything's fine. I do my best to keep up with the daily load."

His big hand squeezed her shoulder. "Never doubted that for a minute, Kiddo." He paused. "By the way, did you get that huge box that was delivered here late Friday? I noticed it was from your folks."

"Oh, yes. Doug brought it to the Wyndhams'. It was a wonderful surprise. They sent some real treats—sugar and ham and tea, a few personal toiletries for me—that sort of thing. I wasn't expecting it, so it felt like Christmas. Isabel cooked us a special meal yesterday in celebration."

"Swell. Well, I'm glad you got it okay. I know how much it means, receiving something from home, even though you know inspectors got the first look at the contents."

"I would've expected that anyway with the war and all." She tipped her head. "They say another box will arrive in time for Thanksgiving. People do celebrate that here in Britain, don't they?"

Uncle Sheldon wagged his head. "Nope, I'm afraid that holiday's exclusively North American. Only our military personnel and the Canadian troops will get to enjoy the traditional turkey dinner with all the trimmings they'd have had back home. The closest thing to that here in England is the special Harvest Thanksgiving service in the churches around the end of September every year. People take gifts of foodstuffs and money to their church in thanksgiving for the harvest of the field, and everything gets donated to charity. That's about it."

"Oh. Well, I think I'll treat the Wyndhams to an American Thanksgiving celebration, since Mother and Daddy will be shipping me another box of foodstuffs. Of course, it would probably be too much to expect a turkey to come the distance without spoiling en route. We civilians can't get in on shipments going to our military."

"I'm sure Isabel and Wilfred would appreciate the gesture. You're getting along with them okay?"

"Oh, yes. I wondered if I would at first. But they're such dears. Even stuffy old Wilfred has his comical moments.

I've grown to love them both."

"Great. I figured you would. They're good people." He glanced at his watch. "Oh, I'm running late. I'd better get outta here before I miss my appointment altogether. I'll check back with you later, Snooks. Take care."

"Right. You, too." Watching after her uncle as he hurried off, Tricia released a pent-up breath. Then, cradling his film against her apron with one hand, she closed the door before flicking the warning light to the on position.

She eyed all the work awaiting her in the various baskets, more interested in developing the shots from yesterday—particularly those of her and Doug—than the usual war photos. But honor prevailed. She started on her uncle's stack. After all, that was what she was being paid to do.

As she clipped up finished prints from the films Uncle Sheldon had previously brought by, it struck her how very young so many of the U.S. soldiers appeared. Did they even shave regularly? Kendall, the big brother whom she'd admired all her life, hadn't been much older than these boys when he'd died. How many of these fine young men would meet the same sad end? Renewed loathing for the Nazis and the Third Reich made her clench her teeth.

Some of Ned's work from the week before, however, revealed that the days he'd been out of the office he must have found transport into occupied France again. Despite his womanizing tendencies, the guy obviously had an adventurous bent. Dora had even mentioned that he'd put in a request for a transfer to North Africa so he could be closer to the real war. No doubt the office would be less lively without his presence if the transfer went through.

Processing the battle scenes—visible proof that the enemy side also suffered losses and death—helped in some perverse way to ease Tricia's anger. But even as she tried to justify her intense dislike for the Germans, an unwelcome realization came to her. Some of those men were probably as young and virile as the ones in the Allied forces; and they, too, must be leaving behind family members and girls who loved them. *You're letting a few too many sermons get through to you, Tricia-girl,* she thought with a grimace, then redirected her concentration to the task at hand.

By quitting time, her baskets had more decorative weave showing than undeveloped film. But she couldn't wait any longer. As her last official act, she developed the roll she and Doug had taken on Sunday, taking her time to make sure each frame was processed to her satisfaction as she relived that delightful afternoon. She did her best not to dwell on the tender rush of feelings when his fingers had lightly brushed her forehead.

"Hmm. You're not half bad, St. Claire," she said under her breath, smiling as she watched his image grow clear and sharp in the yellow safe light. "One might even say incredibly photogenic, and that's no exaggeration." Her eyes lingered on a particularly charming shot of him she'd taken near the lake as he gazed out over the water. It wasn't quite a silhouette, but the oblique angle accented his strong features, while the breeze toying with his hair gave him an appealing boyish quality. She stared at it for several minutes, deciding it was her favorite one of the lot.

The shots of her, on the other hand, she found much less impressive. It had nothing to do with any lack of expertise on his part. She'd just always preferred to be behind a camera rather than be its subject. But her mom and dad would like the photos, no doubt.

She'd discovered that one of the negatives had produced an eerie shot of her image and Doug's superimposed within the same frame. Obviously she had forgotten—or he had—to advance the film when they'd been photographing each other, resulting in a double exposure. Oddly enough, the finished print had them almost back-to-back, each of them gazing off into opposite directions. Their bodies, though still somewhat distinguishable, overlapped in the middle of the frame.

Tricia stared at the photo for several moments, perusing the pensive expressions on their faces. It seemed indicative, somehow, of the two of them and their views of the war. There she was, her hatred for Germany causing a bitter tightening of her lips; and there was Doug, his concern for the enemy as lost souls glowing like heaven's light in his eyes. Giving the photo a last once-over, she dropped it into the wastebasket. Then she removed her apron, turned off the safe light and the outside light, then opened the door.

"It's about time," Doug said, a mischievous grin adding a teasing glint to his eyes as he stepped toward her. "I was just about to give up and head back to the hotel for the night."

"Don't you have anything better to do than hang around darkrooms, St. Claire?" Tricia asked, hoping to match his light tone. In truth, however, his unexpected appearance made her heart skip a beat, made her feel as if she'd been caught doing something she shouldn't have been doing—like talking to his picture. Hopefully he hadn't overheard her.

He shrugged, completely unconcerned. "Hey, I just wanted to drop off today's film, that's all. I don't like leaving it in my desk."

"Oh."

"So it's okay if I take it in there?" He tilted his head toward the darkroom as he turned the knob.

"I'll do it," she blurted out and all but snatched the film sheets right out of his hand. Then she darted around him and went in without bothering to flick on a light while she deposited them in his designated basket.

"What's all the fuss about?"

His voice came from right behind her. He'd followed her!

"Nothing. Nothing at all. I just like to do things myself." But even to her own ears, her answer sounded dumb. Really dumb. Especially since the glow from the hall clearly illuminated her day's work. . .including the photos from yesterday. She cringed when he caught sight of them.

"Well, well. What do we have here?" He turned the light on and moved closer to them, a lopsided smile playing with a corner of his lips.

"They're just from yesterday," she said inanely. "I wanted them to be nice and dry before you saw them." *Not to mention get rid of the worst ones of me*, she added silently.

"Hmm. Not bad. In fact, I'd even say they're great," he mumbled, eyeing each one. "Think I like this one best, though." He pointed to the pose where she'd crossed her eyes. "It shows real. . .character."

"Right. Can we please go now?"

"In a minute, in a minute. I'm not done looking them over just yet." In a slow perusal that sorely tried her patience, he took his good-natured time assessing each one. "I would have to say these are some of the prettiest pictures I've taken since I've been in England. I mean, look at this one," he said, inclining his head toward it. "You've got great cheekbones, do you know that?"

Tricia stood rooted in place. "I'm not even smiling in that photo."

"Yes, you are. Look at those eyes. If that's not a smile, I don't know what is."

She folded her arms and tapped her foot, trying to hurry him on. "Okay, now you've seen them. Let's just leave, okay? They'll still be here tomorrow, and they'll be dry then. They'll look better. . .maybe."

Turning away from the line of prints, he quirked one side of his mouth. "I don't know why you're giving me the bum's rush, but if it'll make you happy. . ."

She didn't mean to meet his gaze, but her eyes seemed to have a will of their own. And one look was enough. She had to laugh—which fortunately broke the tension she'd been feeling.

Doug merely grinned. "That's what I like about you, Tricia. You really know how to cheer a guy up."

❧

The encounter with Doug in the darkroom now a humorous memory, Tricia managed to put it behind her and focus on other things.

After the supper dishes had been washed and put away and she'd listened to the prime minister's nightly address with the Wyndhams, she excused herself and retired to her bedroom. There she composed a newsy letter to her parents to let them know how their shipment had been appreciated by the household.

All her life she'd taken for granted the advantages of growing up in an affluent family. Her wardrobe always consisted of the very latest and best quality fashions, and a generous allowance enabled her to buy anything she desired, whenever she wanted to. Now, living in a nation at war, she was seeing a different side of life. Many little niceties were hard to come by, if not impossible to obtain; yet the mind-set that prevailed among the inhabitants of London centered around giving, not getting. Folks seemed more concerned with making sure those less fortunate were provided for. Tricia found their unselfishness quite humbling.

Slipping out of her clothing and donning her silk pajamas, she wondered what new experiences her college friends had had since joining the various venues of the war effort. Had their eyes been opened to an entirely different set of values, the way hers had? Tricia was convinced that even if she returned tomorrow to her nice safe home back in San Francisco, she would never again look down her nose at people who lacked financial means.

❧

Having finished his nightly devotional Scripture reading, Doug closed his Bible and reclined against his pillow, his fingers laced together behind his head. Here it was, mere seconds after he'd read his customary chapters, and he couldn't remember a single word. Fine lot of good that would do him. But the truth was, his thoughts remained back at work. In the darkroom, to be exact.

Strange, Tricia's attitude regarding the photos the two of them had taken on yesterday's outing. She'd been downright. . . awkward when he'd followed her in there and noticed the finished shots. And it wasn't as if she shouldn't have expected him to be curious about them. Who wouldn't? But he sure would've liked to have been able to take his time and study the ones he'd captured of her. Obviously the gal had no idea of how incredibly beautiful she was, how she eclipsed the very glories of nature. Did she realize her hair was as soft as a fragile butterfly's wings? He let out a ragged breath.

But when had she made the silly face and crossed her eyes? Seated next to her while that kind sailor took those shots of the two of them, Doug had gotten no indication she planned to do anything but smile. In fact, it surprised his socks off that she'd actually clowned around. This was a new facet to the gem that was Tricia. One he definitely liked. A lot. Maybe even too much.

His mirth dimmed. Too bad a real relationship with her was forbidden.

Father, are You getting through to her yet? I'm sensing some kind of inner struggle when I'm with her. I know she goes to church now, even if it is out of sheer duty. But it's a wonderful church, and the minister is one of Your true servants. Keep leading her there, Lord. Instill within him the words she most needs to hear. May every sermon he preaches chip away at the wall of unbelief she's built around her heart until it crumbles completely. Let the glorious light of Your love shine down on her.

I'm trying very hard not to let my feelings get out of hand. . . .

Inhaling a slow, deep breath, Doug cut his prayer off before he uttered a promise he didn't have strength to keep. It was getting impossible to put words to what was taking place within his own heart.

Maybe he was looking forward to seeing her every morning and afternoon a little too much.

Maybe it was time for more fieldwork, time to put a little distance between him and Tricia.

twelve

England had given up on mass daylight bombing runs over Germany early in the war because of heavy losses and now conducted its raids in the dark of night. But the Americans, hearing the Nazis had stepped up production in several of their factories, decided that a surprise attack during daylight hours was of critical import. Doug observed as pilots, bombardiers, navigators, and gunners assembled for their pre-mission briefing at 0530, ready to hear the plan that had been approved by the commanding general. There they got their first look at the target map. The weather, the route to the target, and the route home were laid out as well.

Because of the high risk involved, the raid was assigned on a volunteer basis. "I'm afraid the only escort we'll have will be theirs," came the leader's sober reminder. "If captured, give no information." The grim-faced flight crews who accepted the challenge knelt for a prayer given by the chaplain, then headed for their planes.

It had taken forever for Doug to wade through the drawn-out procedure involved in obtaining clearance to go along and document the mission. But having done so, he changed into the flight suit and fleece-lined boots he'd been given, gathered his camera bag and the other gear he'd been issued—a sixteen-pound flak vest, parachute, and escape kit—and heaved them into the back of a waiting jeep. The public relations officer then drove him to the assigned aircraft and the crew he'd already met at the briefing.

Doug was well aware that his press camera was nowhere near as strong as the built-in type specially designed and used for photoreconnaissance. But any pictures he took would be suitable for news accounts and archival purposes, once they were released by military censors; and he felt confident of his ability to contribute to this mission just as he had the previous one.

The rigger who had issued Doug his parachute had coached him in its proper use. As Doug bumped along in the battered vehicle, he mentally reviewed the procedure, though he hoped and prayed that the chute wouldn't be necessary.

He knew the contents of escape kits varied, but typically contained useful items such as a map made of silk, a tiny compass, caffeine tablets to be used as stimulants, pain medication, some foreign currency, a small hacksaw blade, and his ID and photo. If the plane was shot down and he was lucky enough to get picked up by the underground instead of the Nazis, the latter would be used to forge documents that would help him escape into friendly territory.

Most of the bomber crew had already boarded the aircraft when Doug arrived in the Jeep. He nodded and waved to those waiting to board, then hopped out and retrieved his belongings.

"Good luck," the PR officer hollered cheerfully above the deafening roar of powerful engines warming up. Air from their spinning propellers rippled the grass along the edges of the runways.

"Thanks." He watched the vehicle make a U-turn and drive away. Then he turned to the plane in which he'd be flying, one bedecked with a colorful rendition of a buxom blond resembling Betty Grable. He couldn't suppress a droll smile, yet he found the row of small silhouettes of bombs painted on the fuselage a bit more comforting—proof of its having survived other dangerous missions.

"Greetings, Pal," waist gunner Sergeant Ben Moss yelled, coming to clasp Doug's hand. "We're set to take off once you're aboard."

He nodded and climbed after Moss and his fellow waist gunner, Sergeant Lester Green, into the narrow confines of the bomber's belly. He took the position they indicated, gratified that his own official flight attire made him at least appear as though he were one of them.

"Ever bailed out of a plane before?" Lester Green asked.

"Nope. Never."

"Well, there's no guarantee today'll be your first jump. No sense worryin' about it. These birds can take quite a lot of punishment, and Ben and I'll be keepin' a sharp eye out for the Luftwaffe." He set his oxygen mask nearby until needed and took a fold-down seat beside his fellow gunner.

Doug made himself as comfortable as possible for the take-off. Once they were airborne, he opened the memo pad he'd brought in his kit and began recording observations and sensations as the three dozen planes in the group assembled in the tight formation that provided them maximum protection from all sides.

"Pilot to crew," the captain's voice said over the interphone. "We're at ten thousand feet. Put on oxygen."

As the gunners fastened on their oxygen masks, Doug did the same. The temperature inside continued to drop as the plane forged ever higher; and soon enough, he gave up trying to write, choosing instead to put on warm gloves as the other men were doing. He wondered if Tricia would be upset when she learned he'd gone on another bombing raid. Thankfully, his parents had no knowledge of his choice to put himself in harm's way—they had enough to worry about with one son at sea.

Nearing Germany, the crew put on steel helmets and parachutes and took their battle positions. As the coast came in sight, the formation split into groups to confuse enemy radar and reduce the danger from their aerial armaments. Tension kept the crew on high alert. Soon enough, the first black puffs of flak dotted the sky as the enemy calculated the altitude and speed of the approaching bombers.

Once past the smoky field of flak, distant specks in the sky grew into ME-109s.

"Okay, men. Here they come. Keep your eyes open," the captain said quietly over the interphone.

The Luftwaffe fighters queued up single file like bees and swooped down toward the formation, their guns cutting loose a hailstorm of bullets. The B-17 shook with the vibration of its machine guns returning fire as the swifter aircraft came within range.

Nervous perspiration trickled down Doug's back. He prayed hard and kept out of the way while the guys manning the guns did their utmost to protect the plane.

"Two more fighters diving at nine o'clock," someone said over the interphone.

"We see 'em."

"Another pair at two o'clock," a different voice said.

"Got my sights on 'em."

Bullets peppered the fuselage.

"A B-17 out of control at three o'clock!" someone said in alarm.

Doug swung his gaze to the gunner's window, but from his position couldn't see much beyond the haze of smoke.

"Come on, guys. Get out!" A pause. "See any parachutes?"

"Two. . .three. . .four. There's a couple more."

"Fighter comin' at us in a half-roll, one o'clock."

"See 'im."

When they finally neared the target—rail marshaling yards and war production facilities in Stuttgart—the Luftwaffe's fighters peeled off so ground fire could take over once again. Bursts of black smoke scattered shrapnel into the sky.

"Bomb bay doors open," Doug heard over the bomber's interphone.

"Bombs away!"

Suddenly lighter by a few thousand pounds as its explosive contents plummeted to earth, the heavy bomber rose percep-tibly. Then the heavy bomb bay doors closed. Doug had no problem envisioning factories below being torn to shreds or steam engines and boxcars being hurled askew like miniature toys on mangled tracks.

The B-17 made a turn for home and left the range of

ground fire, only to face the fighters again. Pointless though it was, Doug couldn't help ducking as one of the gunners took a bead on an ME-109 heading straight for them, its guns peppering them.

Up front, a huge explosion jolted the Flying Fortress.

Doug looked toward the cockpit and gasped. A wall of flames!

Moss and Green sprang from behind their guns, frantically waving their arms, while the radioman shot out of his compartment, tightening the straps on his parachute. The tail gunner in his kneeling position behind the tail wheel quickly exited through his escape hatch.

Panicked, Doug yanked off his oxygen mask and pawed at the strings and snaps of his heavy flak vest, trying to get out of it so he could tighten his own parachute. He barely had the thing secured when Moss kicked the nearby escape hatch open and shoved Doug. Moss and the others plunged after him.

In the skies, the battle raged. Swift, agile fighters pursued the remnant of lumbering bombers, whose guns kept up a relentless defense.

Once outside in the cold, Doug felt like he was in a dream, falling through the air on an otherwise perfect autumn day. He could still see the picturesque city of Stuttgart in the distance, beautifully situated in a valley with steeply rising slopes. Just as he felt a fleeting pang of regret that bombs had to mess it up, a lack of oxygen caused him to pass out. When he came around, momentarily, he forced himself to concentrate on the instructions he'd been given.

You'll be over enemy territory. Wait till you're low to the ground before pulling the ripcord. If they spot your chute high in the air, Nazi troops will be waiting when you hit the ground, assuming they haven't shot you first. Hide the chute, and keep yourself hidden for a day or two. If you're not captured by then, chances of making contact with the resistance doubles.

With a thick forest of trees rushing to meet him, Doug yanked the ripcord, and the sudden jolt of the chute springing free startled him. As he floated down, he took note of the landscape below made up of gentle hills, forests, meadows, and vineyards. *Father, may Your will be done. Please protect the rest of the crew, Lord. Be a shield around them. I commit myself into Your hands. Please look after Tricia. . . .*

Tricia arrived at work bright and early, eager to get busy. After greeting Babs and Dora and exchanging the usual chatter, she filled a cup with coffee and headed for the darkroom.

The photos from the day before had dried crisp and clear. A few needed to have the edges trimmed to a uniform size, so she took out the paper cutter and lined them up by the graph lines to keep the cuts straight. Working on the job-related images first, she stacked her uncle's photos neatly to one side, then did the same with those belonging to the guys, making a pile for each of them.

When she came to the personal ones from the outing at Hyde Park, an unbidden smile broke free. "Yep, you're not bad, St. Claire. Not bad at all." With no one there to see her, she took her time cropping each photo and feasting her eyes. "A gal could get used to looking up at a face like yours." Tricia took a deep breath, then slowly let it out.

She discarded one shot of herself she didn't particularly care for; and as it fell into the wastebasket, she thought of the print that had been thrown away the night before. Her curiosity got the better of her. She bent and retrieved the thing, then scrutinized it more closely.

"For a double exposure, it does have a unique and quite interesting charm," she said, thinking aloud. She studied the facial expressions once more. "Maybe it's worth hanging onto after all. And maybe I've been in the darkroom too long," she added on a dry note. "Or else I wouldn't be talking to myself."

With a shake of her head, Tricia stored the personal photos in an available drawer, then clicked on the NO ENTRY light and reached for her apron. Time to get down to business.

An hour before quitting time, she ran out of work for the

first time since she'd started her job in London. With a last critical look at the new batch of photos now drying, she decided to leave her cell and see if perhaps Uncle Sheldon or Doug or even Ned Payne had brought their latest films by.

But the wall basket held no new film sheets or canisters containing exposed rolls. A perfect opportunity to work on the articles she hoped to submit stateside to the Chronicle. Tricia glanced around to find a vacant typewriter. Spying Doug's, she walked to his desk and rolled a new sheet of paper into his Remington.

"Well, this is a first," Babs said, sashaying over to her. "For a minute, I thought our dashing Doug had snuck right past us without so much as a 'How are you, gals?'"

"No, it's just me. I've nothing to do in the darkroom at the moment. Thought I'd do some writing instead."

"It's just a slow day," Dora chimed in from her station. "If something exciting doesn't happen pretty soon, I'll die of boredom. Either that or be called back to the States for lack of news."

"Oh, come now," Babs chided, her freckled face turning impish with a grin. "The guys are all out just now. I'll put on some fresh coffee. Let's not work ourselves into a royal dither when we've not had a chat for ages."

"Good idea," Tricia said, though she'd have preferred not to waste this chance to do her typing. "I'll finish this while the coffee perks. How's that?"

"Jolly good."

The three of them were laughing over a humorous account of the English girl's weekend, when Uncle Sheldon strode in, his face ashen.

Babs and Dora immediately sprinted back to their desks and resumed work.

"Hi, Uncle Shel," Tricia said, sensing something was wrong as she stood to give him a hug. "Sure hope you've brought me some more films. I'm all caught up."

"Huh? Oh, yeah. I do have some, but I didn't bring them

with me." He raked his fingers through his hair. "It's just about quitting time. You kids can go home now," he tossed over his shoulder. "Except Tricia."

"Don't tell me you're tossing me back into the dungeon!" she teased.

A grim foreboding slithered through her as his normally jovial demeanor became deadly serious and he took her by the shoulders. "We need to talk."

"Sure. Whatever you say." Wondering if she'd made some gross error and ruined or lost a critical roll of film, she drew a shaky breath.

"We're out of here, Sheldon," Dora called. "See you tomorrow. Bye, Tricia." Their footsteps echoed through the silent office until the door closed after them.

"Th–this is something the others can't hear?" Tricia stammered.

"They'll hear it, all right. Just not tonight. I'll tell them in the morning."

"What? We're closing down? What? Tell me, Uncle Shel. You're scaring me."

He searched her face, his hazel eyes filled with suppressed emotion. "I don't know how to tell you this, you being his friend, and all."

"Whose friend?"

"Doug's."

A chill went through Tricia. "So this is about Doug? What is it? Has something happened to him?"

"We don't know that for sure. Naturally we're all hoping he's okay."

"Who is we?"

"The commander over at the airfield. Doug went along on a bombing mission early this morning. Several of our planes did not make it back. His was one of them."

"Are you serious?" Tricia gasped, unable to accept the ramifications of what her uncle was telling her. She felt the blood drain from her face.

"I'm afraid so, Honey. According to other members of the mission, the B-17 he was in was shot down by the Germans. Our guys were in the middle of an air battle, so nobody had a chance to check for any parachutes."

"And even if they did," Tricia murmured in a monotone, "the crew would land in enemy territory, wouldn't they?"

He nodded his graying head.

A cold emptiness—one almost as vast and dark and cruel as the one she'd felt when she'd first heard the news of Kendall's death—pressed all the air from her lungs. She felt her knees give way.

Uncle Sheldon caught her and, grabbing the nearest chair, eased her gently down.

"I know you two didn't get off on the right foot in the beginning," he said, awkwardly patting her shoulder in an attempt to comfort her, "but lately the way he talked, you were becoming good friends. I. . .knew you'd want to know."

Tricia didn't trust her voice. Friends. Yes, they were friends. She'd grown rather fond of her tall, handsome reporter. Thought the world of him. Maybe even more. She sagged forward, head in her hands, and rocked, trying to make sense of the news. Doug? Missing? Perhaps even—

"Where's your jacket?" she heard her uncle ask, his voice hazy and faraway in her muddled thoughts. "I'll take you home."

What's the use of going home? What's the use of anything? Her intense loathing for Nazi Germany rose like bile in her throat.

She didn't remember getting her jacket or leaving the office. She didn't remember how she got home. But suddenly she stood before the Wyndhams' house, her uncle's arm around her, supporting her as he knocked on the door.

"Yes?" Isabel said automatically, drawing it toward her. "Why, Sheldon. Tricia." Her face contorted with concern. "Whatever is—"

"I'm afraid my niece has had a bit of a shock," he supplied.

"One of my guys, Doug St. Claire, was aboard a bomber that was shot down over Germany today. I've brought Tricia home."

"Oh, no, no," Isabel crooned, wagging her head. Reaching for Tricia, she wrapped her arms around her. "How frightful. Oh, my dear, dear Tricia. You mustn't give up hope, Luv. We'll pray for your young man in our evening prayers. God will look after him, you'll see."

Tricia wasn't about to remind the kind woman that God hadn't exactly looked after Kendall. She meant well. "Thank you. I—I'd rather just go to my room, if you don't mind. Be by myself for awhile."

"Whatever you wish, my dear. I'll look in on you after a bit."

"Don't feel you have to come to work tomorrow," Uncle Sheldon said quietly. "We can get along without you for a day or two, however long you need."

Tricia gave a nod. Numbly, she crossed the room and climbed the steps to her sanctuary. Her thoughts were so tangled inside her head, she made no attempt to unravel them as she sank to the bed, still in her jacket, and lay staring into nothingness.

I have no reason to fear death.

Doug's strange comment floated across her mind, though now it seemed to take on actual significance.

But Tricia couldn't accept the possibility that he had died. Not Doug. He was too full of life. Too full of his faith.

Faith. How could anyone believe in a God who would allow good men to die while wretches like the evil Nazis and their sympathizers went on and on and on, killing and murdering and ruining people's lives for senseless, insane reasons?

But for the first time in her life, Tricia wished she knew how to pray.

thirteen

Hours melded into a jumbled blur of emotions and sensations that barely penetrated the numb fog inside Tricia's head. Never had she felt so hopeless. So useless. She couldn't cry, couldn't think, couldn't pray. Sleep eluded her through the night; and when sounds below indicated the rest of the household had awakened, she rose and padded across the squeaky floor to peer out the bedroom window at morning's thin light.

Gray clouds as heavy as her heart hung low enough to brush the tops of tall structures in the distance, accenting the forlorn rubble marring every view of London, adding even more oppression to her flagging spirit. Somehow the dreariness seemed fitting.

Not particularly caring about such mundane matters as her attire, Tricia shed the pajamas she'd put on in the middle of the night, then groped blindly in the closet and donned the first thing she touched, a pair of brown woolen slacks. She added the top sweater in the drawer, hoping its warmth might somehow ease the nagging chill that made her insides shiver. After tugging on a pair of thick socks, she stepped into her slippers, set the rumpled bed to rights, then debated about going downstairs.

Isabel's light tap on the door made the decision easier. "We've a nice pot of tea brewing, Tricia, Dear," she said, her voice whisper-soft as if hesitant to intrude. "We do hope you feel up to having a bit of breakfast."

Tricia opened the door with as much of a smile on her face as she could muster. "I don't really care to eat, but a cup of tea would be most welcome."

The older woman placed an empathetic arm around Tricia's shoulders and walked her to the staircase. "Wilfred and I prayed for Mr. St. Claire all through the night. Stormed the very gates of heaven, you might say. We're holding on to the hope that God has your young man in His hand."

Was Doug her young man? Tricia wondered. A kind of friendship had developed between them, an understanding, an acceptance of one another, perhaps. Even a definite attraction. But it was all so new. She'd hardly had time to process her feelings, to see what image might emerge and turn clear as crystal. She knew only one thing: She wasn't ready to lose him.

She mulled over Mrs. Wyndham's words all the way to the kitchen and sank onto the chair the couple had obviously pulled out for her, while Isabel filled her china cup almost to the brim. "Thank you."

Mr. Wyndham looked across the table at her, his faded blue eyes sympathetic and dark-circled, as though used to enduring endless nights of loss with friends and acquaintances. He gave a tentative smile. "Chin up, now. We'll have none of that giving up just yet. The Lord Himself is in control."

"Do you truly believe God knows all about this?" Tricia asked, years of doubt hindering the seed of hope from taking root within her.

His steady gaze did not waver. " 'Tis a fact, my dear. He sees even a sparrow when it falls to the ground. He counts the number of hairs on our heads. All of His creatures are precious to Him."

"Then why. . ." Tricia began, wondering how to frame the question deepest in her heart, "why does He make such awful things happen? Especially to someone like Doug, to whom faith in God is so very important?"

Isabel released a troubled breath and turned from rinsing out dishes in the sink. "Our heavenly Father does not make bad things happen, Luv. However, in His sovereignty, He allows them to take place, in order to bring about His purpose in our lives."

"That is what I do not understand." Taking a sip of the hot tea, Tricia regarded the older woman, then set down the cup.

"What purpose could there possibly be in standing by while a plane—one fighting for the cause of right—crashes, taking almost a dozen good men with it? It just doesn't make sense. And it sure makes me leery of accepting this unquestioning faith you all have," she added, aware of the caustic tone her voice had taken on.

No one spoke for a few minutes.

Outside, raindrops began to patter against the window. Softly at first, then quickly gaining intensity until rivulets of water coursed down the pane. It seemed to Tricia that the very skies wept. She envied the clouds that freedom.

"Well," Wilfred murmured in the heavy silence as he stood to his feet, " 'tis getting late. Best I be on my way. I've a lot to see to today." He bent to bestow a peck on Isabel's cheek before moving to the back door, where he put on the rain gear hanging in readiness. "Take care, now." With a parting wave, which included them both, he took his leave.

The house seemed oppressively silent all of a sudden.

Isabel returned to the table and refilled her and Tricia's cups before taking her customary seat. She poured a dollop of milk into hers, along with a smidgeon of sugar, then stirred the mixture thoughtfully. "We must remember," she finally said, "that God's will is not the only one at work in our world. Satan, the evil one, has been hard at work since before the beginning of time, intent on ruining God's creation. And man, too, has a will that often takes him far from his Creator."

The religious pamphlet Doug had given her had said much the same thing, Tricia recalled, but not quite as simply as Isabel had expressed it. Until now she'd never particularly thought about things from that angle. Yet somehow, in some small way, it sounded logical. She just didn't know why.

"All we can do," her hostess said quietly, "is pray for Doug and trust him into the Father's hands."

Tricia sighed. "I don't really know how to pray." A bitter smile tightened the corner of her mouth. "Guess I never saw much need for it."

But Isabel didn't recoil in shock from that confession. Rather, she tipped her head and smiled understandingly. "All of us must come to God sooner or later, Luv. He teaches His children how to trust Him, how to pray."

"What about those who aren't His children? Those who don't deserve to be?"

Isabel reached over to pat Tricia's arm. "But that's the most wonderful thing about God, you see. None of us deserves His favor, because of our sin. He gives it as a free gift, through His Son, when we accept the forgiveness purchased by Jesus when He died on the cross in our place."

There again came almost the identical thought Doug had related. Tricia continued to study her in silence.

"I've a most wonderful little booklet that might be of help," the older woman said. " 'Tis right in the parlor. I'll get it for you. It may be of help when you go back upstairs and take time to read it through." She rose and bustled away momentarily, then returned with a small leaflet, which she set before Tricia. "Ask God to show Himself to you, to reveal His truth. He always listens to the prayers of our heart."

Tricia perused the pamphlet. *How to Find Peace with God.* Wondering if that, too, would present the same message as the one Doug had given her, she managed a thin smile. She did appreciate her hostess's sincerity. His, too. "Thank you," she breathed, standing and taking her cup to the sink. "I think I'll go up now and lie down again, if you don't mind."

"Not at all, my dear. Not at all. I'll be praying for you, too, along with Mr. St. Claire. I know God will work out His purposes in all of this."

In the quietness of her room, moments later, Tricia set down the booklet and went again to the window. With her elbows resting on the sill, she leaned forward, gazing out at the dreariness, watching puddles overflow in the street and run down into ditches, rushing onward to lose themselves in the Thames or elsewhere.

Did God truly know where Doug was? In the grand

scheme of things, did He care about the fate of one man, one woman? Or was the whole idea the romantic figment of a weak soul's imagination, a mere hopeful dream?

I have no reason to fear death.

Doug's pronouncement drifted across Tricia's thoughts like the refrain of a song never far from her consciousness. His eyes had twinkled when he'd spoken. She recalled his expression, his confidence, his utter sincerity as he'd said the words. Even though she hadn't been able to accept those convictions at the time, she deeply respected them. A small part of her even admired them because inside, in the secret places of her heart, she yearned for the kind of peace that sustained people even in times of crushing sorrow.

And she desperately wished Doug would come back and tell her more, answer the questions his statement raised within her. He couldn't be dead. *Please, God, don't let him be dead.*

Thinking again of the booklet Mrs. Wyndham had given her, Tricia walked over to the bed. Isabel said to ask God to reveal Himself and His truth, that He always hears the prayer of one's heart. Kneeling down, her arms resting on the smooth quilt, Tricia bowed her head and offered the first real prayer of her life—simple, childlike, and halting—yet one she felt from the depths of her being. She hoped it would please Him. Then she opened the book and read it cover to cover, while still on her knees.

&

Two days passed. Tricia could not let herself dwell on thoughts of Doug. Losing him had reopened the wound caused by Kendall's death, almost doubling the anguish she'd only recently begun to live with. But no amount of ranting and raving about life's injustices had brought her brother back. She'd had to accept his death, and the passage of time had eventually enabled her to do so. And languishing around the Wyndhams' house wasn't making the loss of Doug any easier, either. She needed to get busy. Do something. Anything to make the time pass until she learned to function without his charming presence in her life.

She arrived at work earlier than usual that morning. Neither Babs nor Dora had arrived, but she didn't feel up to facing anyone quite yet anyway. The lights were on, an indication that Uncle Sheldon had opened up before heading off to whatever duty needed taking care of. And he'd made the coffee. Taking a cup from the stack of clean ones, Tricia filled it and headed for the darkroom.

As always, the work baskets brimmed over—all but one. Tricia tried not to look at the basket that normally held Doug's undeveloped film; and as soon as fresh developing baths were readied and the temperature of each was at the proper level, she focused on making a dent in the mountain that her uncle had turned in.

It felt good to be busy again. Though not completely at peace, Tricia sensed that hope was near, almost within reach. She'd about memorized the booklet Isabel had given her, as well as the words of the similar pamphlet from Doug. Over the last few days, she'd derived a peculiar comfort whenever the older woman offered prayers in her presence. Most amazing of all, Tricia found herself actually anticipating Harvest Thanksgiving Sunday and the church service that would go along with it—a real first in her life. *Even if the minister reverts from the theme of the day to another sermon on forgiveness,* she thought wryly. For some reason, a lot of things were beginning to make sense.

All except the war. Watching the various scenes of death and destruction coming into view in the developing baths, Tricia detached herself from the realities of each image and let her professional side labor at bringing out the sharpness required to reveal the best qualities of the scenes.

As she worked, however, she couldn't help seeing things in a new light. If ever she'd needed proof of the sinfulness of mankind, as mentioned in the pamphlet, it was right in front of her eyes. Maybe the minister was right. Maybe the only way to endure the horrors of war was to forgive, rather than let bitterness control the rest of one's life. No doubt Doug would have forgiven the enemies who'd shot down his plane. Maybe it was even possible for her to find that same forgiving spirit.

By lunchtime Tricia was ready for a break. Her back ached, her neck had a crick in it, and her eyes were bleary from staring long and hard at every frame. She deposited her apron on her work stool and went out to face the world.

"Oh, hi, Luv," Babs called from across the way as she slipped into her coat. "So glad to see you back. We were just about to run out for a bite. Would you care to join us?"

Dora, not quite so prone to jumping in where she might not be wanted, merely smiled hopefully while removing her purse from a desk drawer.

"Why, yes, thanks. My stomach's been growling for some time."

Outside, the threesome walked in silence for half a block.

"We missed you," the British girl said at last. "Ned's transfer came through. Paul's only been in once all week. The place has been frightfully dead without you and—"

Babs covered her mouth with her hand. "Sorry. I'm always speaking out of turn."

Tricia squeezed her friend's shoulder. "It's okay. Really. None of us expected that plane to be shot down. It's natural for things to be. . .subdued around here. It's going to take all of us awhile to get used to. . .the change."

"Please know you're in our prayers," Dora offered. "You and Doug both. I wasn't much of a churchgoer myself until now. This hit pretty close to home."

The statement made Tricia's throat grow thick. Fortunately the roar of a military transport precluded any response as it chugged past them and turned the next corner, the rowdy American GIs waving madly and blowing kisses their way.

When they arrived at the restaurant, they found the typical crowd almost split the seams of the Pigeon's Roost. But just as the girls entered, the boisterous group from one table took their leave. Babs dashed to claim it, and the three of them stood to one side until the waitress cleared the clutter from her previous customers, then set out menus.

Strains of a popular song somehow managed to filter through the hubbub: "I'll be seeing you in all the old familiar places. . . ."

Tears sprang to Tricia's eyes. She quickly blinked them away and tuned the music out as she gave her full attention to choosing an item from the list before her. "I'm not as hungry as I thought. Think I'll have the soup," she announced a little too brightly.

"Not me," Babs declared. "I'm ready to devour a fat slice of shepherd's pie. How 'bout you, Dora?"

The slender blond toyed with a wisp of hair as she studied the menu. "No, I believe I'll have fish and chips. I've had a strange hankering for it ever since Ronnie told me it's another favorite of his."

"Oh, you are too, too much," Babs said, giggling.

"So, you two are becoming serious?" Tricia asked, looking over the top of her menu.

Dora blushed slightly. "Well, one never knows. It's hard to make plans with the war going on around us. Ron's regiment could be called up at any time." She paused. "Maybe that's why things feel so urgent between us. We're afraid to waste a moment."

Tricia wondered if she had wasted a few too many moments in her life. Maybe she should have encouraged Doug a little, been more receptive to his overtures. Then he might not have gone on that last mission. . . .

"Just wait till I tell you what happened to me the other day," Babs chimed in, obviously attempting to keep things cheerful. "I met this Yank over on Piccadilly, see? Not exactly a dream or anything. But something about him was so frightfully appealing. Next thing you know, he tells me the story of his life, how he's so homesick he could go AWOL. I felt so sorry for the bloke, I ended up inviting him home for supper with my parents. He and my dad hit it off jolly well, I might add."

"Do tell," Dora teased. "Next thing we know, you'll be talking wedding bells."

"Hardly!" Babs protested. "He's already got a fiancée back in the States."

Tricia had to smile. Somehow, being out among people in a normal setting bolstered her spirits a little, and she was glad the girls had invited her to tag along with them. More proof that life goes on, she reasoned. No one can do anything to change what has happened. The best any of us can do is to press forward, a day at a time, making each moment count.

No matter how empty and useless it seems.

fourteen

The moving observance of Harvest Sunday now behind her, Tricia threw herself into her work over the next few weeks, careful to maintain a pleasant, somewhat-cheerful attitude before the Wyndhams and her coworkers. But all the while, deep inside her, yawned a deep, empty chasm into which she struggled to keep from plunging headlong.

Her hometown newspaper, the *Chronicle*, had responded to her query with enthusiasm, so her waking hours brimmed with activity, keeping her too occupied to dwell on morose thoughts. Whenever she had time to work on the photo essay she'd entitled "Faces of Courage," she focused her attention on assembling a layout of suitably organized pictures of varying depths and widths. She hoped the result would be a coherent narrative made up of still shots whose meaning would be apparent to a viewer at a glance. Meanwhile, she wrote poignant vignettes about interesting common folk she met on weekend jaunts around the city and submitted them to wartime censors for clearance before cabling them to the paper.

But the nights of solitude were hardest to bear—the long dark hours after the Wyndhams had turned in, when the only sound in her bedroom was the small clock ticking on Margo's nightstand. The quiet regularity of the beats would finally lull her to sleep in the midst of her heavy, sad thoughts.

There'd been no word of Doug or the rest of the crew that had gone down over Germany with him. The staff at the newspaper headquarters judiciously avoided mentioning his name in her presence or, for that matter, the incident itself. But to Tricia their silence seemed easier to bear than if they'd patted her on the shoulder and mouthed overly optimistic assurances about his being alive. Surely someone would have heard something by now, if even the slightest possibility of his existence remained.

It was time to let go and get on with her life. To be thankful for the short time Doug St. Claire had been part of it. Such a charmer, he'd been. A true friend. Until she met him, she had never entertained thoughts of domesticity, getting married, and presenting her parents with the grandchildren they craved. She'd concentrated only on avenging her brother's untimely death and, while doing so, establishing a reputation as a photo-journalist. Now even those goals seemed unimportant, super-ficial. Other things of far more importance called her, things she was trying desperately to discern.

One night, alone in her room, she switched on a lamp and reached for the religious pamphlets Doug and Isabel had given her. They were creased now, their pages long since having worked free of the staples holding them together, and the faded printer's ink was barely legible. Tricia didn't mind. She knew them both by heart. She was weary of avoiding the truth, of going her own way. She sensed the time had come for her to give her heart and life to God, to allow Him to make the choices that would affect her future.

Releasing a long, slow breath, Tricia slid to her knees beside the bed. "Dear God, I'm not sure if this is the proper way to do this," she whispered, "but I know I have sinned against You. I've been hateful and vengeful and made many bad choices. I ask Your forgiveness for all those things and pray that Jesus will come into my heart and be my Savior. And from this moment, I give over control of my life to You. May everything I say and do honor You always. Amen."

There on her knees, an incredible peace flowed through her being, one beyond words. Humbled under the awesome calm that infused her, Tricia felt immediate release from the weight of hatred and sorrow that had bowed her shoulders and stolen her joy. She no longer felt it was up to her to avenge Kendall's death. Nor did she feel so alone. God was with her now to bear her above the circumstances surrounding her, no matter what happened. A tremulous smile broke forth as she rose and crawled into bed.

For the first time since hearing the news that Doug's plane had been shot down, Tricia slept like a baby.

❧

"So what do you say?" waist gunner Ben Moss muttered. "Think you'll be up to putting some weight on that leg pretty soon? I'm anxious to get outta this cave. The place is crawling with Nazis. The longer we're stuck right under their noses, the more likely we are of being captured."

Doug glanced at his splinted leg, propped before him on a makeshift footstool deep within the sheltered cave. Even in the flickering lantern light, his shin looked huge, swathed in bandages in lieu of a proper cast. He hadn't made the most graceful of landings on that first parachute jump three weeks ago. Even now, he could hear the sickening crack his fibula had made in protest of being the primary shock absorber on that unbelievably sudden impact. Only by the skin of his teeth had he managed to contain the blood-curdling howl he'd needed to let out, releasing a grunt instead. Over the next several days, he'd used up his and his buddies' supply of pain medication from their escape kits. "It's getting there. The medical student Frieda brought by says in time I'll be as good as new."

"Won't be too soon, that's for sure."

"Hey, God is in control," Doug reminded him. "How else would we have escaped capture until our rescuers came along and ushered us to this four-star hiding place?"

"Yeah, yeah, I know. But if it was up to me, I'd hustle the plans along for sneaking us out of here. Get to Switzerland and back to jolly old England. I've had enough of German hospitality. I just wish the rest of the crew could have made it here with us."

"Well, there's nothing we can do about the others who survived. Maybe they'll get by okay in the prison camp. I'm praying they will."

"But it's taking forever for Frieda and her brothers to come up with false documents for you, me, and Les."

At the sound of his name, the other waist gunner rolled over on the pallet where he'd been dozing. He raised groggy eyes. "What's up?"

"Not much," Ben said. "Just the usual griping."

Lester Green, looking about as unkempt and unappealing as his fellow cave mates, rubbed a grubby hand over his unshaven chin and yawned. "Well, keep it down. No sense givin' away our presence." He paused. "Wonder when supper's comin'. I'm starved."

Doug's stomach growled at the mere thought of food. As his companions lapsed into silence, he closed his eyes and reflected on God's mercy. As thick as the enemy troops had been the day the plane had been shot out of the sky, only God's angels could have kept the three of them from being rounded up like the rest of the surviving crew members he'd seen get bound and marched off to become prisoners of war.

Definitely answered prayer, he decided. Letting his gaze roam the dreary interior of the secluded, manmade cave etched into an embankment within the thick forest, Doug felt as much at peace as if he'd been lounging back at his hotel. Only the steady ache of his injured leg reminded him that he and the other two men were still in peril. The painful fracture had prevented them from being whisked out of the area at the first opportunity.

He breathed a silent prayer for protection for Frieda Dengler and her two brothers, Karl and Reinhardt, three valiant believers motivated to join the resistance because of pamphlets printed by an underground organization known as the White Rose. Thanks to the efforts of its college-student founders and volunteers who refused to accept the hateful Nazi ideology forced down the throats of the German people, hundreds of Jews and downed Allies had been rescued from certain torture and death—and in almost all cases, they had been spirited to freedom.

Of course, being confined on his back for this long stretch of time had provided Doug with plenty of prayer time. He spent some of it interceding for his family and his sailor brother, but far more prayers went up for Tricia, hoping that God was still at work in her heart. It would be ten times harder to keep his distance from her when he got back to England, because against his noble intentions, somewhere along the way in establishing a cordial relationship with her, his feelings for the sable-haired beauty had grown far beyond the boundaries of friendship. He couldn't imagine setting eyes on that gorgeous face of hers without spilling his guts and proclaiming his undying love. And if, by some miracle, she had given her heart to the Lord, the difference in their faith would no longer be a factor.

On the other hand, if she still had qualms about "getting religion," as she put it, he'd do his best to remain only a friend. Anything to have her in his life. Even if he had to keep his distance. He'd do it somehow. He released a ragged breath.

A shuffle from the direction of the cave entrance announced the return of their rescuers.

"You are hungry, ja?" golden blond Frieda said as she came into view, opening her oversized coat to reveal bulging pockets. Rosy cheeks from the nippy fall temperature accented her fair skin, making her appear years younger than her early twenties, especially with her hair in braids.

"Some bread ve bring," her younger brother Karl announced. "Und cheese. Fresh apples, too." Handsome and muscular at twenty-one, only haunted eyes that had witnessed far too much belied his youth.

Reinhardt, a serious-faced, freckled lad of seventeen, with the same strong Aryan features as his siblings, whipped out a thermos of coffee and began filling chipped cups the men used.

"You are all godsends," Doug marveled. "How is it you are able to move so freely out there, with so many enemy forces about?"

"Practice," Frieda said. "Much practice ve haff at being

careful. Und Gott is mit us. Many times ve are almost caught."

"You've got me almost ready to believe all that religious stuff you two spout from your soapboxes," Benny Moss confessed. "Between you and Doug, here, we've been getting it from all directions."

The young woman's cheery smile grew broader. "Is goot, to believe. Ve pray for you. All of you." Her gaze encompassed the group.

Doug accepted the bread and cheese and offered a quick prayer of thanks as they passed the food around to the other men. He bit off a huge mouthful, his hunger making the simple staples taste as delicious as steak and potatoes.

"How is da leg today?" Frieda asked, tilting her head to peer at the splint.

"Doesn't hurt quite so much."

"Goot. Is getting better, I tink. Tomorrow I try to contact Heinrich at Marien hospital to check it again. Ve must not keep you here much longer."

Doug gave her an understanding smile.

"All clear," Reinhardt said quietly, returning from the entrance. "Da patrol is gone now. Da dogs I do not hear."

"Den ve leave," his sister said, buttoning her wrap once more. "Better ve not stay long. Ve come back vhen ve can."

Nodding, Doug offered the threesome a salute. "God be with you."

"Und mit you," Frieda murmured, her clear blue eyes lingering a fraction on him, but not quite revealing anything. Then she turned and left.

"Once I set foot in merry old England again," Ben said wistfully around a chunk of bread lodged in his cheek, "I'm gonna have me the thickest, juiciest steak I can find at the first restaurant I come to. With mounds of mashed potatoes and brown gravy. Maybe some apple pie."

"Not me," muttered Lester. "I want some fried pork chops. Mashed potatoes'll do fine, of course. Apple pie, too. I can hardly remember the last time I had such a feast."

"What's your pleasure?" they said in unison, swinging their gazes Doug's way.

A slow smile stretched from ear to ear. "All of that sounds pretty good. But at the moment, the only feasting that appeals to me will be done by my eyes when I gaze upon a certain lovely gal I left back there."

Ben let out a subdued hoot, and Lester chuckled.

But the more Doug thought about the idea, the better he liked it.

✌

Another package from California arrived in mid-November, filled with wonderful food items and rare goodies. Tricia promptly wrote to Margo, asking her to come home for a visit and share a real American Thanksgiving.

Sure enough, the daughter of the house breezed in a day or two early. Her mother had yet to return from making canteen rounds, and her father was involved in a meeting several blocks away. But Tricia had just gotten in from work and was about to start supper when her friend arrived.

"Tricia! So good to see you again," Margo exclaimed after setting down her suitcase and grabbing her in a huge hug. "It's good to be home. We've been so busy, of late, I nearly missed the opportunity to approach my boss and request time off."

"Well, we're glad to have you back for however long your superiors allow. I've tried not to completely take over your bedroom."

"Oh, pshaw! We'll have none of that now. I rarely need use of the thing. I'm glad somebody's around to look after it and keep it clean." She paused and swept a glance around the house. "Mum and Dad aren't here?"

Tricia shook her head. "Not at the moment, but I'm sure they'll be back soon. Guess I don't have to tell you to make yourself at home. Do come into the kitchen and sit down. I'll put on some tea."

"Tea? We still have some of that luxury, with the rations and all?"

"Sure do. Thanks to my parents. They insist upon keeping us supplied with treats as long as I'm here." Crossing to the stove, Tricia set the kettle over the hottest area and scooped loose tea into the tea ball in preparation for the boiling water, then set some cookies onto a plate and brought it to the table.

"Mm. Biscuits," Margo remarked. "I think I love your parents. They sent some of these to Kenny once." She sampled one of the sugary treats. "What's been happening in your life? Anything exciting? Anyone exciting?"

Tricia joined her at the table and claimed the chair opposite her. "Not really. For awhile I kind of thought there might be. One of the guys from work." Her throat closed up, and it took some effort to get the rest of the words out, flat, unemotional, in a rush. "The plane he was in got shot down about a month ago. There's been no word."

"Oh, of course. My parents did mention that dreadful news in a letter. I'm so sorry." The slender blond reached for Tricia's hand, her sky blue eyes clouded with concern. "I was hoping you'd received some hopeful news since then."

"No, there's been nothing. It's okay, though. I've. . .come to know the Lord since it happened. He's helping me through the sad days."

Margo's eyes misted over and she smiled. "I don't know what to say, Tricia. I'm positively thrilled to hear you've found peace with God. That helps tremendously, making things easier to bear. But I also know just how much it hurts to lose someone special."

"Of course you do."

Her friend's expression suddenly brightened. "Well, perhaps it was never meant to be for us to become sisters-in-law, but it would seem God had a plan to bind us together in an even better way. We're sisters in His family. Eternal sisters. Nothing will ever come between us now."

The very thought flowed through Tricia like a warm wave, but didn't diminish the bittersweet wish that Kendall might have stayed alive and married his sweet English love and brought her to the States to meet their parents. Needing a change of subject, she redirected the conversation. "So what have you been up to, way up north? Anything exciting happening in your life?"

Margo tipped her head, a faint blush cresting her cheeks. "There is a chap who's been showing a bit of interest. A captain in the RAF. Utterly smashing. But I've been leery of becoming involved with another pilot. It's too difficult—all that waiting and weeping. Anyway, I still compare everyone I meet to Kenny. I don't think I could go through that sort of loss again."

"I know what you mean. None of us can afford to plan ahead. Even I have grown weary of this war. I'll be glad when it finally comes to an end. I'm just hoping that we'll all be able to get back to normal then."

"Whatever normal is. We'll have to practically rebuild our poor old England. The way things are—"

The front door opened just then, interrupting the thought. Isabel hastened into the kitchen. "Oh, my darling daughter! You've arrived!" she gushed, bending to kiss Margo's cheek.

"Hello, Mum. Tricia seems bound and determined for me to experience Thanksgiving, as she calls it. So I've brought my wondrous presence home for a few days."

"Splendid. Anything that brings you to us is more than welcome. One more reason to give thanks." She beamed at Tricia. "Is that tea you've got on, Dear? How nice."

"It'll be done in a jiffy. Take off your coat. Sit down and tell us about your day."

Isabel removed her wrap and draped it over a chair back before taking a seat. " 'Twas rather ordinary, I'm afraid. Just the usual serving sandwiches and coffee. But I did meet quite a number of interesting individuals in the shelters. Some of them mentioned an American reporter—a young woman—who's been taking photographs and inviting them to share their experiences."

Tricia suppressed a blush. "I do hope I haven't been overbearing. I try hard not to be offensive or pushy."

"Not at all. They spoke quite highly of you. According to them, they now have a greater respect for America and Americans in general, no matter how the young soldiers conduct themselves away from home."

"Well, they still embarrass me," Tricia admitted as she filled the teapot and brought it to the table. "I've even had the occasion to tell a few of them off in my travels. They can be so rowdy and boisterous and rude!" She collected cups and saucers from the cupboard and set them out, along with a pitcher of milk and some sugar.

"There's not much we can do about the behavior of young men far from the influence of their parents," the older woman said. "But soon enough they'll be face-to-face with enemy forces. None of us should begrudge them a reasonable bit of enjoyment beforehand. After all, they've made quite a sacrifice, coming here to aid us in our battle."

"I kind of like them," Margo teased. "They're such a chipper lot. Marvelous fun to be around."

Tricia appreciated her friend's optimism and overall cheerfulness as she talked and reveled in having Margo home once more. Now that her newfound faith made them sisters in the Lord, she looked forward to an even richer, deeper fellowship between the two of them. One that would help make up for what she'd lost in Doug.

At least a little. She swallowed and forced a smile as she poured the tea.

fifteen

Delicious aromas mingled together in a tantalizing blend as Tricia labored over the Thanksgiving meal. In appreciation for the Wyndhams' thoughtful care during her stay, she banished the older couple from the kitchen so she could wait on them for a change. Their daughter, however, she allowed to help. Besides, she hated to waste a minute of her friend's visit.

"I only wish this could have been a turkey," she told Margo wistfully, opening the oven to baste the clove-dotted ham with pineapple glaze one last time. "It's so much more traditional. And there could've been delicious bread stuffing, the whole bit."

"Please, don't be sad," her friend coaxed, slicing celery stalks for the relish tray. "Turkeys and other fowl are quite impossible to obtain here anymore; and after months and months of meat rations, this lovely meal will be a most welcome treat. I know we've rarely had cranberry sauce or homemade pumpkin pie. It'll be marvelous." She arranged the cut celery sticks artfully beside the carrot sticks and olives on the cut-glass platter.

"I didn't think my mom and dad would bother fussing over a huge holiday meal, now that there's just the two of them at home," Tricia said, "but they wrote that they'd invited our next-door neighbors over to share the feast. That family recently lost a son at sea." The remark drove home the reminder that she'd never have another Thanksgiving with her brother. And now that she was a Christian and felt the deeper meaning behind the day, the knowledge of how wonderful it might have been to share it with Doug compounded the ache in her heart.

"I should've loved to meet your parents. Kenny thought the world of them. And you, of course. Special occasions made him quite homesick." Margo paused and plucked a stray bit of carrot peel from her ruffled apron. "What else needs to be done?"

Tricia collected her fragmented thoughts and glanced at her. "I suppose you can take the warm rolls to the table while I fill this bowl with mashed potatoes. Everything's about ready to be put on."

Taking the meat platter to the dining room moments later, Tricia cast a critical eye over the array of food adorning the table and breathed a prayer of thanks that she hadn't burned anything, not even the candied sweet potatoes. She hoped her British family would enjoy the meal. Removing the apron, she smoothed her blouse and skirt and waited for the rest of the household.

Margo summoned her parents and grinned when their eyes widened with pleasure as they approached the feast waiting in readiness.

"Everything looks delicious," Isabel murmured, taking the chair Wilfred pulled out for her.

"Fit for King George himself," he supplied.

Tricia exchanged a smile with Margo, and the two took seats, then looked to the man of the house to return thanks.

"Our most gracious heavenly Father," he began, his voice thick with emotion, "we are humbled by Thy goodness and watch care over us. We praise Thee for this incredible bounty supplied by our American friends and ask Thy blessing upon them and upon this special feast. May we remain conscious of Thy hand in the affairs of mankind this day. We ask these things in the name of Thy beloved Son. Amen."

"Amen," the others echoed.

"I suppose I am to carve this wonderful ham now," he said, rising and picking up the carving knife and fork. "Though it seems a shame to render such a piece of art into slices."

After the care she'd expended in scoring the top into perfect diamonds and inserting cloves just so, Tricia beamed at his appreciative comments as he cut several generous portions.

Isabel started the vegetables on the rounds by helping herself to a dollop of fluffy mashed potatoes and passing them to Tricia before reaching for the glazed carrots.

"So tell us," Mr. Wyndham said, filling his plate with portions of everything, "how exactly did this custom get its start? You did say it's an annual event, as I recall."

"Oh yes," Tricia replied. "It began within the very first year of the settlement of Plymouth Colony. The harsh Massachusetts winter had claimed nearly half the original settlers, but the coming of summer renewed the hope of those who'd survived. The Indians had taught them how to plant corn; and after the first harvest, the colonists wanted to offer thanksgiving to God for sparing them. Their Indian friends provided wild turkeys and venison, and everyone ate together in a grand feast. And so began the yearly tradition, now celebrated annually in November."

"Well, 'tis a lovely one," Isabel said. She buttered a roll and bit into it, chewing thoughtfully. "I should like to add a British touch to it, if I may, by having each of us express something for which we are particularly thankful at this time. I shall start by stating my own gratitude for God's bringing Tricia into this home. You are quite like another daughter to us, my dear, and have brought a house that was far too lonely back to life."

With her emotions banked so near the surface, Tricia had to blink away the tears that sprang to her eyes.

"And I," her husband said, taking up the thread of conversation, "am thankful for the recent military victories we've been hearing about on the nightly broadcasts of the *London News and Review*. Stalingrad has managed to hold, Morocco has fallen, the Yanks and British forces are advancing in North Africa. And crowning it all, El Alamein has capitulated thanks to the valiant efforts of our own brave hero Montgomery. The Germans are no longer a threat to Egypt. Perhaps victory is indeed a bit closer this day." He forked a chunk of ham into his mouth.

"Hear! Hear!" Margo chimed in. "I am particularly thankful

for my new precious sister in the faith and for knowing she is here to look after Mum and Dad when I cannot be. I could not have asked for a sweeter friend—though having known her brother well, I should have expected it."

Deeply touched by the love expressed by her English family, Tricia could barely speak. She had to take a sip from her water goblet to bolster her control. "I have many things to be thankful for. When I first arrived in Britain, my heart was filled with hate for Germany and all its people. I had no room in my life for God. But He brought many dear people across my path who showed me by example what it's like to be a Christian. I am most thankful that because of their faithfulness—your faithfulness—He was able to break through my defenses and bring me to the place where I could accept His Son as Savior and Lord of my life. I've never known such peace."

"That is wonderful," Isabel breathed. "I think this tradition, Thanksgiving, is a truly splendid one. I should like to celebrate it every year from now on, Lord willing. Even after this horrid war, when our dear Tricia leaves us to return home to California."

Gazing around the table at the sweet folks she had grown to love, Tricia felt her heart swell with joy. Only one thing would have made the day more perfect, but she couldn't allow herself to dwell on him.

Tricia was filled to bursting by the time the pies had been served and raved over and the mess had been cleaned up. Her ears rang with the pleasant conversation the family had shared. She and Margo finally hung the damp kitchen towels and retired to the bedroom.

"Let me tell you," Margo gushed, "that was a delightful meal. Thank you for including my family in your tradition." She dropped onto the bed and leaned back a little, propping herself up by her arms.

"It was as much a treat for me as it was for all of you," Tricia assured her as she kicked off her shoes. "And it kept me from being homesick. This is the first year I wasn't home with my parents for the holiday."

"Well, it's something we won't soon forget." She yawned. "By the way, I brought something with me to show you. Some photos of Kenny and me. Would you like to see them?"

"Oh, yes. Very much."

Margo rose and walked to her suitcase, then returned to the bed, a leather-covered album in hand. After sitting down, she patted the quilt beside her, and Tricia joined her.

"This was taken on one of our first dates," Margo explained after opening it to the first page. "We'd gone to watch the changing of the guard, just like tourists. It was such fun."

Tricia perused the photo, staring at the brother who had been taken from her in his prime, the brother who would forever remain young in her mind. "I noticed the palace guards are dressed in khaki these days," she commented.

"Oh, of course. They've been wearing that since the beginning of the war. It does look quite strange not to see them in red coats and tall black hats, doesn't it?"

"Where was this one taken?" Tricia asked, admiring a shot of Kendall lounging on a huge rock surrounded by flowers.

"In Hyde Park, actually. That was a marvelous summer day. The flowerbeds were an absolute riot of color."

Tricia smiled. "You two made a great couple. How sad things turned out the way they did." She sighed and slowly examined the remaining pages before closing the cover and handing it over to Margo. "Thanks for sharing them. It was almost like seeing him again."

"If there's any photograph you especially like, I'd be pleased for you to have it."

"Really? I wouldn't want to take one that meant something special to you. Why don't you choose one for me of the two of you. Then I'll be able to remember you that way. Together."

"As you wish." Reopening the book, Margo flipped through the various candid shots and pried one loose from the photo corners with a fingernail. "Will this do? I feel quite strange offering a rather amateur picture to a professional photographer."

"It's perfect." Tricia eyed the snapshot. The last thing she would have done was analyze the quality of its composition. "I couldn't have made a better choice. Thank you."

"I don't suppose you have a picture of your friend from work," Margo said hesitantly. "Doug, right? I never had the pleasure of meeting him."

A bittersweet mixture of sadness and joy flowed through Tricia. "Yes, I have several. From a day the two of us were at Hyde Park. I happened to have my camera with me at the time." Reaching for the nightstand drawer, she opened it and removed the photos she'd brought home after her first day back at work. Unable to bring herself to look at them, she handed them without comment to her friend.

Margo took her time studying each one, then at last shook her head. "Ohh. Such a dreamboat. A fine catch, as they say." She looked up at Tricia as she returned them. "You know, I've no actual reason to be saying this, and perhaps I'm speaking out of turn. But I wouldn't give up all hope that he's alive. Not yet. It could be he's someplace where it's simply impossible to get word to you."

"But how could that be? Surely there'd have been some mention of at least one member of that crew if any of them survived. It's going on two months now."

The shrug of a shoulder accompanied Margo's thin smile. "Stranger things have happened. After all, God knows exactly where Doug is. And He still works miracles, even these days."

Tricia gazed down at the top snapshot in her hand, and Doug's smiling face blurred behind a sheen of tears. "I'm trying. Truly I am. But with each day that passes, my hope shrinks a little more." Despite her resolve, tears flooded her eyes and rolled down her cheeks.

"I know," Margo crooned, slipping an arm around Tricia's shoulders and hugging her. "I know."

❧

One day ran into the next in the cave, until the guys lost track of how many weeks had passed. But they knew the drill. No lights after dark, and no unnecessary talking. There'd been another air battle that night in the skies nearby, with sounds of exploding bombs in the distance and the relentless pounding of ground fire shaking the very earth. It seemed to last forever. Then the drone of the aircraft receded, the firing lessened and died away, leaving an intense quiet that was unnatural. Surreal.

Outside, night patrols combed the area in search of downed airmen. Having been in that precarious position himself, Doug relived the scene in his mind: flashlight beams and powerful searchlights on military trucks jabbing like ice picks through thick bushes and groves of trees, sweeping across vineyards and open fields. Fierce dogs, straining at their halters, sniffing out unfamiliar scents. Himself scrunching up into a ball and almost holding his breath, waiting for the inevitable. . .

Father, be a shield about our men, Doug prayed. Keep them under Your wings, safe from harm. Don't let anyone but the resistance find them. He was well aware that individuals affiliated with the White Rose and similar underground organizations were in every bit as much peril as any of the Allies. Maybe even more. No mercy was meted out to the valiant souls connected with the resistance. They wouldn't be taken to some horrible prisoner-of-war camp if caught. They'd face execution. *Protect Frieda and her brothers, Lord. They're doing all they can to help the righteous cause.*

His stomach growled in the stillness.

"Thanks for the reminder," Benny muttered under his breath. "I was trying not to think about food."

"Sorry."

"I hope our resistance friends have done a thorough job of hiding the entrance to this cave," Lester whispered. "Those last shouts sounded a touch too close, them and those mangy dogs."

"Pipe down," Doug warned. "No sense broadcasting where we are."

The three lapsed into silence again. Only their breathing punctuated the air.

Absently Doug rubbed at his splint. Maybe the itching meant his leg was healing. In any event, it was driving him nuts. Trying to ignore the nagging irritation, he let out a long breath and rolled over in the darkness, forcing his thoughts to a more pleasant subject.

What would Tricia be doing now? He didn't even know what time it was or what day of the week it was; but since it was dark, she'd probably be home at the Wyndhams'. He imagined her curled up in that comfortable parlor, perhaps listening to music or news of the war on the radio. If he lived to enjoy such simple pleasures again, he'd never set foot inside another B-17 or reconnaissance plane.

And if he could just lay eyes on Tricia's expressive face once more, he'd ask for nothing else.

sixteen

December crept in like one more draft, its bitter temperatures inflicting a rash of sore throats and colds to already unhealthy Londoners. Fortunately, however, the government relaxed the restrictions on the use of heating fuel. That ruling did much to assuage the ill feelings against the American troops, who could only be billeted in homes with central heating and were, as was pointed out, in much better health than their British hosts.

Cold wind and icy rain mixed with snow often made navigating the roads on a bike treacherous, so Tricia bundled up and switched to picking her way to the newspaper office on foot. After work, before starting for home, she detoured to nearby shops to look for Christmas gifts for the Wyndhams.

She found slim pickings in the stores, though. Because of the need to use coupons to buy clothing, many folks resorted to answering advertisements for secondhand items of apparel to replace things they needed. People muttered about the shortage of fowl for their holiday dinners, and dried fruit for the traditional puddings and pies was so scarce it required a forbiddingly high number of points to obtain.

"I'd planned to wrap up a bit of tea and sugar I've put by and give it to me neighbor," she heard one woman complain to another as the two passed by her in one of the shops. "But the Food Ministry declared it's now illegal to give away rations. Can you believe such a thing?"

" 'Tis just dreadful, that's what it is," her companion agreed. " 'Twill be another grim Christmas this year. Have ye seen the price of toys? And not even new ones, mind ye. I can't see how we'll manage to buy the children anything at all."

Watching the pair move on, Tricia shook her head sadly. A

recent letter from her mom related that the list of rationed items in America was also growing by the month. But few people back home really knew what it was to do without. Not the way these Britons did. It distressed her that even the Wyndhams, who had once enjoyed fine clothes and elegant food, were looking as ill-dressed as everyone else.

"Hi, Babe," an unfamiliar voice crooned from behind her. "How 'bout you 'n me goin' for a drink?"

Tricia turned around, eyebrows hiked, to see a young American sailor, a hopeful grin on his skinny, boyish face.

"No. Thanks just the same." She returned her attention to the heavy sweaters she'd been perusing. One looked just the right size for Wilfred to replace the one he'd recently worn through at the elbows.

"Hey! You're American!" he blurted out.

"That's right," she said evenly, not bothering to look at him.

"Swell. I mean, that's even better. Where're ya from?"

"California. San Francisco, to be exact."

"Well, what d'ya know? I'm from L. A. We're neighbors." He whipped off his cap. "My name's Mike Pierce. What's yours?"

Recognizing that the kid wasn't about to go away anytime soon, Tricia let out a resigned sigh and turned to face him. "Tricia Madison. I'm here with the American press."

"No kidding. A reporter. What d'ya know about that. Say, would ya let me buy ya a cup of coffee? There's a little joint right down the street."

"I. . .don't think so."

"Aw, come on. Please? I won't try anything fresh. I just wanna talk to a gal without an accent for a couple a minutes. What d'ya say?"

Unable to resist the hangdog look in his big brown eyes, she finally relented. "I suppose it wouldn't hurt. But I can't stay long."

"Swell. After you." He gave a gallant bow of his head and indicated for her to precede him. As they stepped out into the elements, he slapped his sailor's cap atop his light brown crewcut, jammed his hands into his coat pockets, and adjusted his stride to match hers. "Wait'll I tell the other fellows I met a gal from home."

"This your first time in England?"

"My first time anywhere," he admitted. "I finished boot camp a couple weeks ago, then got sent here. The place is one big icebox, huh? I haven't stopped shivering since I got here."

Tricia smiled. "How old are you, anyway, Mike?" she asked, liking the young man despite his having tried to pick her up. She flipped the end of her scarf over her shoulder and hunkered into its warm folds.

He puffed out his chest. "Eighteen. And a half."

She chuckled inwardly, thinking he was probably somebody's baby brother just out of high school. No doubt he had parents back in Los Angeles who were worried sick about their boy gone off to war.

"Well, here we are," he announced as they approached a small café. He opened the door for her, then followed her inside the toasty warm but dimly lit interior fairly packed with servicemen and couples. They took opposite seats in a tattered booth. Popular music from American big bands blared from a radio, considerably raising the noise level of the place.

Over cups of coffee, they chatted about L. A's warm Mediterranean climate and sunshine and how carefree life had been back home in California, before the war interrupted everything.

"Say, this has been nice," Mike said after draining the last drop from his cup. "Real nice. I'm glad I met you, Tricia Madison. And it didn't even cost me a pair of silk stockings!" he added with a sheepish grin.

"Silk stockings?" she gasped. "You have silk stockings?"

"I sure do." He patted the front of his pea coat. "Two pairs."

"Can I buy them from you? I need them for Christmas gifts. It's impossible to buy any in the stores these days."

He eyed her, an almost worshipful expression on his face. "Nope. No way. But I'll give 'em to ya."

"Oh, I couldn't—"

"Sure you could. Anyways, I can always get more," he added with a conspiratorial wink. He dug inside his inner pocket and produced the treasured hosiery, each pair wrapped in tissue.

"That's really sweet of you, Mike. Thank you so much." She stowed them inside her purse, then looked up at him with a smile. "Then, in return, I'll give you a tip. Don't try to impress an English girl by calling her 'Babe.'"

The tips of Mike's ears reddened to the hue of a candied apple.

"Treat her nice, like you've treated me," she went on. "With respect, the way you'd want some guy to treat your sister. Okay? You'll find that works much better."

"Will do," he said sheepishly. "Thanks. I appreciate the advice." Rising, he offered a hand and assisted Tricia to her feet, and they went out into the waning daylight's chill.

"Thank you for the coffee," she told him. "It was nice talking with you."

"Same here." He grinned again. "Wait'll I tell the guys. See ya, Tricia." With a jovial salute, he turned on his heel and strode away, whistling as he went.

Tricia smiled after him, thinking how much younger she'd felt during the past half hour, the weight of the last depressing months lifted from her mind. She glanced at her watch. Barely time enough to make it to the Wyndhams' before dark. But having the two precious pairs of stockings in her purse buoyed her spirits so much, she didn't care that she'd have to hurry. She wished she'd bought that sweater for Wilfred while she'd been at the store, but that could wait for another day. Breathing a prayer of thanks at her good fortune, she set off for home at a brisk pace.

❧

"You must leave here," Frieda said, not taking time to offer them the food bulging in her pockets. "Now. Is safe no more."

A jolt of alarm shot through Doug. The shallow height of

the cave was almost sufficient for the two shorter waist gunners to stand but had precluded any attempt of his to try putting weight on his injured leg as yet. "How about taking Ben and Lester with you and leaving me behind? I'll just slow everyone down."

"No way," Benny said. "If one of us goes, we all go."

"Ve help you valk," Karl, the sturdier of her two brothers assured him. "Ve haff cattle truck at home. Ve hide you until ve get papers und move you to new place."

"Where's that?" Lester wanted to know.

A pointed stare and the threesome's silence were the only reply.

"Reinhardt is telling us ven the patrol is gone," Frieda said quietly. "Then ve haff only ten minutes to get deep in da voods before dey come back. Must be no talk. No noise. Yust follow."

The men had only the warm flight suits and leather flight helmets they'd worn when parachuting from the plane, plus the small escape kits to tuck into their pockets—no other belongings to worry about leaving behind as evidence that Allies had been there.

Doug cast a worried look about the dimly lit hovel that had sheltered them during the months they'd been in hiding. God had kept them safe thus far. Surely He would see them through whatever lay ahead.

"Now!" Frieda's kid brother whispered urgently from the entrance.

Ben and Karl positioned themselves on either side of Doug and helped him up, then each put a shoulder under one of his arms and supported him as they started for the exit. He ignored the slight dizziness he felt at standing for the first time in weeks—and the throbbing pulse in his shin. At least it didn't hurt. Yet. He tried to suppress the grunts required by each ungainly step he took with his good leg.

Frieda extinguished the tiny lantern that had provided light.

A blast of winter air whipped about them as they emerged

into the open. Falling snowflakes pelted their faces, stinging like pin pricks. For a second, Doug feared their tracks would surely give them away. But then seeing how heavy the snowfall was, he realized all traces of their movements would disappear quickly. And Reinhardt, bringing up the rear, was already brushing their trail away with an evergreen branch.

Doug had been barely conscious when the others brought him to the cave; and now, concentrating intently on not being dead weight for the two men, he was unable to see much of the landscape in the falling snow. But the pristine ground cover softly illuminated some gentle hills with steeply rising slopes in the distance. He saw they were headed toward a thick forest.

Within moments the little group entered the seclusion of the woods. The thickness of the trees and the heavy storm clouds overhead effectively blocked any moonlight from aiding their escape, so all Doug and the others could do was trust their champions and keep close as they steadily picked their way through the tangle of trees, occasionally flicking on a flashlight to check their bearings. Snow already on the ground from a previous storm and the whistle and whine of the wind through the branches muffled the sounds of their movements.

How long they trudged through the woods, Doug could not judge. His hands, hanging limp over Ben's and Karl's shoulders, were numb from the cold. Even his face felt numb. And the splinted leg he tried to keep elevated as they went felt like it weighed a ton. He longed to stop. Sit down. Rest. But they plunged onward. Ever onward.

He couldn't even pray. The effort of trying to walk wore him out. He was starved and lightheaded and wished the guys would just drop him and go on, let the snow cover him up for good. But then Tricia's face floated across his consciousness—those expressive blue-green eyes and that wry smile of hers—and renewed determination flooded him. He had to keep going. Had to keep going.

They plodded on forever, covering an interminable distance.

"Not far now," Karl whispered at last.

Doug had never heard sweeter words.

Now and then, off in the distance, they glimpsed patches of golden light through the trees. Windows. Of a house. Chimney smoke curled up into the falling snow.

Just before they emerged from the sanctuary of the forest, Frieda raised a hand and halted, and everyone else stopped. "I go on ahead. See dat it is safe."

The tempting sight of that wonderful farmhouse nestled against a semicircle of trees was almost more than Doug could endure as the rest of them waited in place for her signal. His gaze drank in the picture postcard scene as pretty as a Courier and Ives painting, snow falling on the slanted rooftop and the outbuildings. He made out the bleating of sheep not far away. *Please, Lord, don't make us have to sleep in the barn,* he pleaded silently. *I'm so cold.* Even as that admission poured from his soul, he felt himself shiver.

"Is all right," Karl said softly when his sister motioned for them to come. "You be varm soon."

"Sounds good to me," Benny said under his breath.

They covered the remaining distance in a few moments, Ben and Karl stepping lively through the accumulating snow, with Doug half-limping, half-dragging a path between them. They all but carried him inside, where an unbelievably wonderful blast of heat made his face burn in a most enjoyable fashion. The delicious smell of real food filled his nostrils.

An older couple, plump as a pair of Bavarian salt and pepper shakers, rose to their feet at the supper table and beamed at their arriving guests.

"Our parents," Frieda said, indicating her balding, silver-mustached father and moving closer to her mother's round little aproned figure. "Dey speak no English."

"How do you do," Ben and Lester said with dubious smiles as they exchanged nods with the man and his wife.

Doug merely sank to the wooden kitchen chair Karl nudged

out for him with one foot.

After Frieda disposed of their coats, she invited everyone to be seated, then bustled about getting plates for the group. Her father dished up generous portions of thick sausage and potatoes and passed them around, while her mother set out sliced bread and fresh butter.

At home and in their element, the sons of the household became much more animated and chattered exuberantly among themselves and with their father in their native tongue.

Doug, beyond starved by now, almost forgot to return thanks. But catching himself just in time, he bowed his head and said a brief prayer.

"You stay mit us," their blond rescuer informed them as they delved into the meal. "Soon Karl drive you to another safe house. Ve are not far from Switzerland border here. Only a few hours' drive."

A few hours' drive! Doug railed inwardly. Man, that was plenty far enough. And if a couple of good blizzards dumped snow on the mountain passes, that would make a hard climb for a one-legged reporter. *I'll need one more miracle for God to get us to free soil.*

After each of them polished off second helpings, Frieda's mother served warm apple strudel and strong black coffee.

Doug doubted he'd ever tasted anything so good. "Danke schön, Frau Dengler," he said, using up his entire German vocabulary in one fell swoop—and pleasing the woman immensely as he did so.

Now that he was beginning to come back to life, Doug observed with interest the tidy surroundings. A high shelf on the wall opposite the big cookstove sported a row of carved wooden figures, mostly animals, alternating with hand-painted plates. Beneath it, a cuckoo clock lent a cheerful air as it chirped nine times.

Just off from the homey kitchen, in the adjoining room, he glimpsed plump cushions topping a sturdy wood-framed sofa and matching chair that looked incredibly comfortable after weeks on a hard pallet. A woven tapestry scene hung on the wall above the couch, its rich colors accented by the warm glow from wall lamps on either side. He could easily picture Frieda and her siblings growing up in such a place as this. But how they managed to get involved with the resistance, he had no idea.

After all possible pleasantries had been attempted and exhausted and the men's appetites were sated, their rescuers moved the table aside. Then the man of the house pried open a door so skillfully cut into the plank floor, it was nearly invisible. It opened to a secret room, where they would spend this night. . .and who knew how many more.

"Even vay out here is not always safe from Gestapo raids," Frieda explained. "Fader built dis hiding place for dem needing to escape Germany. Many times, it serves us vell. You find all dat you need."

His two companions descended first and lit a lamp, then helped Doug. He looked around and was pleasantly surprised to see great-looking cots with feather pillows, an assortment of food items, and fresh water.

"What d'ya know," Lester said cheerfully. "All the comforts of home."

The floor above was set back into place.

Feeling a kind of security they hadn't known in the cave, Doug had no qualms about giving in to his exhaustion. He eased himself down onto one of the beds and lofted a prayer of thankfulness heavenward, pleading for safety and blessing to fall upon this wonderful household of people who put others' lives above their own.

He'd get back to England soon, Lord willing. Back to Tricia.

seventeen

Midway through December, Tricia's uncle Sheldon gathered his dwindling office staff together for an announcement. He stood before them and cleared his throat. "Now that most of the action's centered around the offensive in North Africa, things have kinda slowed down for us. No sense in you gals sitting here twiddling your thumbs when you could be baking Christmas cookies or out finishing your shopping. Why don't you take some time off?"

"Even me?" Tricia asked, puzzled. "There's always film needing to be developed."

He gave her a tired smile. "Yeah, well, I can always get hold of you if things get desperate. It's not like I don't know my way around a darkroom, Snooks."

"Well, I'm sure not going to argue with you," Dora assured him. "My work's caught up. I'll leave the latest batch of articles in the basket for the Reuters guy to dispatch for me."

"And I just need to straighten my desk," Babs said, her cherubic face alight.

"Fine," he said with a nod. "Then be off with you. Of course, should the enemy resume dropping bombs in our backyard, as folks have been expecting, hightail it back here. Otherwise, I'll see you all after the holidays."

"Swell!" Babs exclaimed, adopting the American word bandied so liberally about Britain. "Happy Christmas, then."

"Yes," Dora agreed. "Merry Christmas."

"Same to you." Without further word, he retired to his domain.

Although the other girls made quick work of their last-minute details and took their leave, Tricia wound up her own affairs at a more leisurely pace. Then she poured two coffees and took them with her to the large private cubicle that made up her uncle's office.

Seated behind his unusually neat desk, with his shoulders in a decided slump and his tie loose and askew, he looked up at the sound of her footsteps. "You still here?"

"Thought you might like some coffee." She placed a cup before him, then sank into one of the two seats opposite him. She studied him for a few seconds. "Something wrong, Uncle Shel?"

He grimaced and exhaled a little huff through his nostrils as he leaned back in his swivel chair. "Naw. I just don't like holidays. They're a pain. Bah. Humbug. All that rot."

Tricia had to smile. "Oh, so that's it. You're homesick."

His hazel eyes lacked their usual merry sparkle when he reached for his cup and met Tricia's gaze over the rim. He took a swallow of the hot brew. "This is the third Christmas I've been stuck a million miles from Maudie. The third one that she and I won't be together. I hate it. I'll miss her fussing around, overdecorating, baking up a storm. . . ."

"I'm sorry," she murmured. "Have you called Auntie Maude lately?"

He nodded. "Yeah. She's miserable, too. I could tell by the fake cheerfulness in her voice. She sent me a package, though. Some fruitcake and stuff I can use now and a box I'm not supposed to open till Christmas morning."

"That was sweet of her."

The shrug of a shoulder indicated his response.

"Well, you don't have to be all alone on the holiday. Come to the Wyndhams'. We'll be having a nice dinner, and Margo will be there. We'd love to have you. I'd love to have you. My family's back in the States, too. We're all we've got here, you and I." The reality of that thought made her heart ache, but she tamped down her sadness.

Some of the tension appeared to ease from his posture. He tipped his head. "I'll think about it."

"Do come," she urged. "Please, Uncle Shel. For me."

He chuckled. "You know, for such a little thing, you sure drive a hard bargain."

"I try. We'll expect you then." Feigning her brightest smile, Tricia stood and went to gather her belongings. But she couldn't leave without swinging past her uncle's cubical one more time. "I left the chemicals in place. They were fresh this morning."

"Great. I'll look after things here. See ya."

"See ya. Take care, now." Thoughts of sharing the holiday with her uncle cheered Tricia as she adjusted her scarf and gloves and stepped out into the damp, biting cold of another winter day.

As she started toward the stores, leaden clouds overhead looked ready to burst. Any moment the sky could explode with fluffy snowflakes, like feathers from a pillow fight. Christmas was still two weeks away. But with any luck at all, London would have a white one, just like Bing Crosby sang about in his new movie.

She imagined her mother back home writing out dozens of colorful cards, wishing friends and loved ones a joyous season. But inside, Tricia knew that neither of her parents gave any credence to the true significance of the coming holiday—God becoming man and coming to earth to redeem His fallen creation. A baby born to die as sin's perfect sacrifice. A lot of Christmases had come and gone before she'd realized it herself. Tonight she'd write them a long letter telling them about the newfound faith that sustained her through sadness, loneliness, and wrenching loss.

Rather than acquiesce to depression, she focused on the shops just ahead. It would be great fun looking for a special present for Uncle Sheldon. So few of the locals could afford the appalling prices attached to even the most simple items. But her salary, supplemented by occasional checks from her parents, allowed a freedom for which Tricia was extremely thankful. She hoped her host family would like the gifts she'd chosen for them that even now lay under her bed in their festive papers and bows.

She arrived home laden with parcels and set them down while she hung her coat and scarf on the hall tree. Then she breezed into the parlor, her splayed fingers ruffling errant snowflakes from her hair.

Isabel, darning in her rocking chair, glanced up from her stitching and checked the mantel clock. "My, you're a bit early."

"Yes. My uncle decided things are too slow at the office right now. He sent us all home."

"How nice. I wish Wilfred could be so fortunate. But alas, he's swamped with trying to find flats for newlyweds and others in need. There's such a waiting list, the slightest opening is snapped up before a sign is posted in the window."

"So I've heard. Is there anything I might do to help you? You've got canteen duties again this evening, am I right?"

She nodded. "But there's no sense in both of us venturing out into the snow, is there?"

"Why not? I like to be useful. . .and we'll get done in half the time, working together."

Mrs. Wyndham's expression softened with pleasure. "If you insist. I would rather enjoy having your company, my dear. And I'm sure your appearance in the shelters would be most welcome by those you've befriended."

Tricia gave a nod. "Then it's settled. I have a few things to take upstairs to my room just now. And I'll be working on a letter to my parents. Give a holler when you want to leave."

"There's no hurry. We'll go directly after teatime."

"Great." She tripped up the staircase to the bedroom, where she wrapped the new things she'd purchased and stowed them with the rest of her bounty. Never before had she appreciated the wondrous privilege it was to give gifts. . .nor had she had friends so sorely in need of being lavished with material goods. And added to that, Margo would be home on Christmas Eve. Tricia found herself anticipating the coming holiday more by the hour.

She made several attempts at composing the letter, wadding each sheet of stationery and tossing it into the wicker wastebasket beside the desk. Then she bowed her head and prayed that God would sort through her jumbled thoughts and help her to express what she wanted to say. Where to start? Idly, she tapped the pen on the desktop and relaxed.

Dearest Mom and Dad, she wrote at last. *I have found a new Friend. I didn't want another day to pass without telling you both how different my life is. . . .*

Once she started, the words poured from her heart as she related how she'd once allowed bitterness and hatred for Germans to rule her every waking moment and how God had replaced them both with faith and love.

> *I've come to realize that I wasn't truly living before I met the Lord. I was only existing. I can truthfully say that I am an entirely different person now, and I view things in a whole new way. Life itself has much more meaning. Even in this war I see His hand at work in the affairs of man, and I know that God is in control. No matter what happens, He will be with me. I will tell you more about my newfound faith in future letters. Meanwhile, please know that you are both in my heart and in my prayers. I love you bunches.*
>
> *Hugs and kisses,*
> *T*

After signing her stylized initial, she folded the papers and tucked them inside an envelope. *Please work in their hearts, Father. Make them hungry to know more.*

"Tricia, Dear," came Isabel's call from downstairs. "Teatime."

"I'll be right there." She slipped back into the shoes she'd kicked off and hurried below.

❧

It had been several weeks since the three men had reached the hideout in the German farm. Doug lay awake in the December darkness, listening to his pals' intermittent snores. He had no idea what time it was, but movement on the floor above the hidden room indicated the sheepherder must be up and about his morning chores already. Just as he yawned and turned over, he heard the table scrape aside. The door opened, and dim light from the bare bulb in the kitchen spilled into the hideaway.

"Come," Frieda said quietly, her tone urgent. "Ve go now."

Go? Doug thought. *Where?* But he roused his sleeping mates at once. "Get your boots on. Looks like we're outta here."

"Rats," Benny groused, tugging socks onto his feet and jamming them into his worn boots. "Just when I was dreaming about me and a gorgeous dame."

"Yeah, well this is for real," Doug replied.

"They say where we're goin'?" Lester asked, slipping into his warm coat.

"Nope. Ours is not to question why and all that. Let's not hold the good man up."

His two companions preceded him up the ladder, while Doug took a quick glance around to make sure they had all their belongings. Then he ascended after them, favoring his sore leg.

"Is no time to eat," Frieda said, giving each of them a wrapped packet. "Fader is loading da sheep. Go to truck. Hurry."

The first cold fingers of dawn were lighting the eastern sky through the trees when the three emerged from the warm farmhouse into the frigid air. Outside they found their host and his elder son funneling a dozen sheep up a ramp into the open bed of a sorry-looking vehicle.

"Does this crate even run?" Lester muttered under his breath.

"Dis vay," Karl instructed, motioning with one arm toward narrow wooden boxes constructed lengthwise along each side of the truck's bed. "For tools und feed," he explained. "But mit false bottom."

"Great," Benny said sarcastically. "We're to leave here in wood coffins."

"Whatever it takes," Doug rasped. "Shut up and climb in."

Quickly they got aboard, stepping lightly around the wooly creatures crammed together in the open space. Ben and Lester, clutching the packets Frieda had pressed into their hands, situated themselves end-to-end in one box, while Karl and his father quickly positioned the false bottoms over them and heaped tools and other paraphernalia over them.

Doug, envying those smaller guys, wedged his broad shoulders into his own compartment and waited for his German rescuers to get to him.

The bed swayed with Karl and his father's movements as they threaded their way through the fat critters to his side. They hoisted up the fake bottom and moved it into position above him. He closed his eyes to keep out any dust or splinters.

Gradually he became aware of the drone of engines in the distance growing noticeably louder.

Another vehicle was nearing!

Karl and his sheepherder father spoke urgently in their own tongue as they hurriedly filled the compartment above him with grain and who knew what else.

Doug held his breath as the sounds became sickeningly recognizable.

Motorcycles. Trucks. Swooping upon the farm!

They screeched to a stop. Shrill whistles pierced the still-dark morning. Booted feet charged the sheepherder's truck.

Then came the shout he most dreaded. "Halt!"

❧

"I say, Mum, the house looks marvelous!" Margo stomped snow from her boots before setting foot inside the entry. Then she set her suitcase down and shrugged out of her heavy coat, her azure eyes drinking in the festive touches. "You've gone all out to make it appear at its Christmas best."

"Quite," her mother declared, trying hard to keep a straight face. "Our dear Tricia wouldn't have any less. We've been doing our best to humor her."

"And loving every minute of it," Tricia teased, coming up

behind the older woman with a hug. "You did tell me I was to feel right at home, as I recall."

"I did indeed. And truth be known, I've rather enjoyed getting out all the cartons of decorations, making it seem like Christmases past, before this horrid war business spoiled everything."

"We're all going to forget the war—even if it's just for tomorrow, one day," Tricia announced. "Welcome home, Margo." Overjoyed to have the daughter of the house back for a few days, she hugged her, too.

" 'Tis good to be back in London. The train was absolutely packed with travelers going home for the holiday."

"I'll help take your bags to the bedroom," Tricia offered, "and then you can help your mom and me finish trimming the tree."

"Splendid. Here you are." Margo handed her a bulging sack to carry, then grabbed the handle of her suitcase, and they clomped up the stairs. "The bag is full of presents, but I've not had time to wrap them yet."

"No problem. I'll help you later. Let's not keep your mom waiting."

After they returned to the main floor, Tricia led the way into the parlor, stepping around open boxes of decorations Isabel was rummaging through. She tried not to laugh at the pathetic tree Wilfred had convinced one of his relatives out in the country to part with. Once it was dressed for the occasion, it would probably look fine, she assured herself.

"Your father unraveled the string of lights for us, so we wouldn't have to mess with that," Isabel remarked. "We'd best put the garland on next, then we can start hanging the ornaments."

"Jolly good plan," Margo said cheerfully. "I'm so glad you waited for me to help."

A goodly supply of laughter interspersed the chatter as the three labored over the spindly fir, bumping elbows and occasionally even heads. At last they stepped back and assessed the finished product.

"I call it done," Isabel said, tilting her head back and forth thoughtfully.

"Beautiful," her daughter breathed.

"Couldn't be more perfect," Tricia had to agree.

The older woman gave a nod. "Then, while you two stack the empty boxes against the wall, I'll put some water on to boil. I'd say we've earned ourselves a nice cup of tea."

"And something to go with it," Margo added. "What are all those delicious smells? You've been baking, if I'm anyone to judge."

Tricia smiled and slipped an arm around her friend's slender waist. "Why don't you come and see for yourself?"

As they took seats in the homey kitchen and Isabel fussed about, brewing tea and arranging an assortment of baked treats on a pretty plate for them all to enjoy, Margo related humorous tales of her latest experiences.

Tricia sat back, listening to her friend's cheerful banter, watching Isabel fluttering about like a mother hen. Uncle Sheldon would join them for the most special of days, on the morrow, and the family would partake of a wonderful dinner. Her heart swelled with joy. In a way, now that she appreciated its significance, this Christmas would be her happiest ever.

But there was no denying. . .it would also be her saddest.

Margo shifted in her chair and focused directly on Tricia for a moment before speaking. "I was thinking you and I might pay a visit to Kenny's grave while there's still some daylight," she said tentatively. "We've no flowers to take, of course, but I thought perhaps a small evergreen bough would suffice."

A surge of alarm throbbed in Tricia's heart.

"It won't be quite as hard as you imagine," her friend added softly. "It's rather peaceful there. I think you need to come with me."

Aware of Isabel's scrutiny and Margo's steady regard, Tricia felt her reluctance give way. "You're right, I know. I really do need to go there."

Within the hour, as a crisp, snow-laden wind toyed with

their scarves beneath the winter-gray skies, she and Margo stood side by side before her brother's final resting place, each of them holding a sprig of fragrant pine. Neither friend spoke, but no words seemed necessary as Tricia gazed sadly down at the small patch of snow-glazed earth, one simple white cross among endless rows of others. So many fine, brave men gone from the world forever.

When she'd first come to England, she'd envisioned herself collapsing in tears on the ground that covered her brother and wailing with rage and grief. But now, aware of God's loving arms bearing her up and the fact that she would be united with Kendall again one day, she felt indescribable peace instead. He was in the presence of his Savior, where nothing would ever hurt him again. She and Margo knelt and placed the evergreens lovingly at the base of the cross that bore his name, then clasped hands and offered a silent prayer. A tear fell to the earth as Tricia raised her lashes, and she saw that her friend's eyes were moist as well. It came as no surprise that neither of them could speak.

At last Margo brushed snowflakes from the top of the cross with her gloved hand and stood. Tricia put a fingertip to her lips and kissed it, then with a wistful smile, touched it to Kendall's name in farewell. Her friend had been right to coax her to visit Kendall's grave.

But as they walked hand in hand toward the cemetery's exit, one niggling thought assaulted Tricia. Doug had no final resting place for her to visit.

eighteen

Tricia awakened before the rest of the household stirred, and impatiently she lay still so as not to disturb Margo. Yesterday's insignificant snow flurries had ended almost as quickly as they'd begun, so the likelihood of the holiday dawning crisp and clear above a pristine blanket of sparkling white was a bit too much to expect. Still she itched to get up and peer out the window in the thin morning light and check it out. Instead, she forced herself to relax by concentrating on God's awesome love for mankind in sending His beloved Son to the world.

How could I have been so blind for so long, Father? I can't thank You enough for finally opening the eyes of my heart. Please bless this dear, sweet family that has made room for me in their home. May they have a truly special day today as we celebrate the wonder of Christmas together.

Beside her, Margo drew a deep breath and rolled over. She yawned and stretched, then blinked sleep from her eyes. "Morning," she said, her voice husky from sleep.

"Good morning. I hope I didn't wake you."

"Hardly. WAAFs always rise at the crack of dawn. Duty, you know."

"Oh. Well, since we're both awake, why don't we go start breakfast? Surprise your parents."

"A capital idea." Flinging the quilts aside, Margo sat up and swung her legs to the floor. "Do dress warm. The first order of business will be to stoke up the fire and heat this place. Want to be first in the loo?"

"No, go on while I make the bed."

Moments later, dressed and eager in their conspiracy, the two of them sneaked down the stairs, careful to avoid the steps that squeaked. Margo, used to the procedure, quickly got the stove and furnace going, then put water to boil for tea. Before Tricia finished mixing a batch of scones, welcome warmth filled the kitchen and began to permeate the rest of the house.

Their ministrations didn't remain secret for long. Isabel soon padded into the room, her feet in thick house slippers, a robe tied about her regal form, and her graying hair in a thin braid down her back. "What are my lovely girls up to?"

"Nothing much," Tricia said, crossing to give her a hug. "Just a little surprise."

"Merry Christmas, Mum," Margo added from the counter, where she dished out bowls of tinned peaches.

"Well, isn't this the grandest thing!" the older woman remarked. "I think I rather like being surprised, to say nothing of being waited on hand and foot. I shall go rouse your father. He'll not want to miss this."

But breakfast preparations were only the beginning for Tricia and Margo. No sooner had that meal been cleared away before it was time to start on the holiday dinner. Wilfred had somehow managed to obtain a real treasure from another of his country relatives—a half dozen Cornish hens, which the girls dressed and stuffed for roasting, along with a goodly supply of whole potatoes. And there were rolls to bake, carrots to glaze, and holiday pudding to chill. Glancing at the mince pies they'd made earlier, Tricia was glad her uncle would be coming to share the day, someone from her real family.

Her thoughts drifted heavenward, and she wondered if Kendall would be enjoying a Christmas celebration with the angels and the saints of God. The mental picture brought a smile to her lips.

"The tree looks lovely today, did you notice?" Margo asked as she cut celery into sticks for the relish dish. "But I hardly expected to see such a mountain of gifts under it."

Tricia slanted her an impish smile. "I guess Santa's elves worked overtime."

"No doubt," her friend chided.

In honor of the occasion, the dining table wore Mrs. Wyndham's best lace cloth, and she insisted it be set with her good china and heirloom silver. Margo added a centerpiece she'd fashioned from small evergreen branches, pinecones, and red bows, a tall red candle on either side. The pine fragrance mingled with that from the decorated fir and an assortment of larger beribboned boughs placed around the parlor.

A knock on the door announced Uncle Sheldon's arrival, and Tricia met him with a hug as he stomped his rubber boots clear of snow that had begun falling again and stepped inside.

"Merry Christmas!" she said. "May I take your coat?"

"Sure thing, if you hold these." He held out a box of chocolates he'd brought for the household to enjoy and a bag of small gifts.

"You're too sweet," she said, kissing his freshly shaved cheek, chilly from outside. "We were only expecting you to bring yourself."

"Yeah, well, a guy has to buy something for somebody, right?"

"I suppose. Go right on into the parlor. Isabel and Wilfred are already there. I believe he's got a checker game set out and waiting for you. I have to help Margo."

As she set down his gifts and returned to the kitchen, she heard her uncle's boisterous greetings to the host and hostess, and his cheerfulness bolstered her own spirit. Quite an improvement from the depressed man she'd left on her last day of work. Yet she fully understood what it was to be lonely—particularly on special occasions, when loved ones and families gathered together to celebrate and share memories.

Perhaps this Christmas would leave the two of them with memories they would treasure forever, even if they were deprived of their very dearest loved ones.

"I think everything is ready to be put on the table," Margo said, her voice rescuing Tricia from tumbling over the edge of sorrow's abyss. "Perhaps we should set the hens on each plate, rather than passing a heavy platter round. What do you say?"

"Sounds fine to me. You do that, and I'll bring in the rest."

When the family gathered for the meal, Christmas carols and happy holiday music poured from the parlor radio. Tricia's throat tightened at all the joyful expressions and beaming faces. She bowed her head while Wilfred offered a particularly touching grace:

"How we do thank Thee, our precious Father, for the indescribable love this wondrous day proclaims. We thank Thee for the gift of Thy beloved Son, for His unspeakable sacrifice, and for this opportunity to gather as a family to fellowship around the table. We ask Thy holy blessing upon this beautiful meal and upon the beautiful hands that so lovingly prepared it for us to enjoy. May the coming new year find us ever faithful in service to Thee. We ask these things in the name of Jesus. Amen."

Whispered amens echoed among the group. Then Wilfred began passing the various food items around.

"This sure looks delicious," Uncle Sheldon commented as he filled his plate. "Smells good, too."

"The girls have been laboring over it all morning," Isabel told him. "They wouldn't allow me to so much as lift a finger. I'm afraid I'm becoming quite spoiled." She placed a delicate slice of butter on her bread plate before passing it on.

"No more than you deserve, if you ask me," he returned.

"You two may discuss the meal all you like, but I'm anxious to see what exactly is in all those boxes beneath the tree," Wilfred said, a mischievous grin twitching across his lips. "It looks as if someone bought out the shops." He forked a morsel of meat into his mouth.

Tricia feigned an innocent look. "It was all the work of Father Christmas, I believe. I heard he arrived in a B-17." As soon as the words left her mouth, her appetite vanished. The others chuckled, but she could only sip water from her goblet and hope such sad reminders wouldn't steal the joy from the rest of the day. *Please don't let me fall apart, Father. Help me to be conscious of my blessings.*

Somehow she managed to do justice to the remainder of the food on her plate. But aware of how fragile her emotions were, how tentative the barrier holding them back, she didn't dare dwell on dreams that could no longer come true. Fortunately, the cheerful music, always a boon to her spirit, perked her up.

"I should say we're ready for some of that pie I've had to endure smelling since last night," Wilfred announced. "Though I must admit, the torture has been most exquisite."

"It won't take a minute," Margo said, putting her linen napkin aside and rising. "Trish and I will have the table cleared in short order." Her sky blue eyes, sparkling and smiling, met Tricia's.

"Right." She also stood and began collecting plates and empty bowls.

At the end of the dessert course, Uncle Sheldon patted his stomach with a slightly pained grin at Tricia and Margo. "You two sure know your way around a kitchen. I may not eat again for a month!"

"Yes, it was truly delicious," the elder Wyndhams agreed.

"Let the dishes sit awhile," Wilfred suggested, "and we can all retire to the parlor. We've a bit of a ritual we enjoy before delving into the waiting presents: the reading of the Christmas story to remind us of the greatest Gift of all. Our daughter can do the honors this year."

Tricia followed the others; and while Isabel and her husband chose their customary rocker and upholstered chair, she took a seat beside her uncle on the sofa.

Margo took the old Bible down from its shelf beside other treasured volumes and opened it to the well-known passage, then smiled and began reading in her pleasant, airy voice. " 'And it came to pass in those days, that there went out a decree from Caesar Augustus, that all the world should be taxed. . . .' "

Listening with her heart, Tricia admired her friend. Daylight through the windows, aided by the glow from the multi-hued lights on the tree, cast a lovely aura over her golden blond pageboy. And her peaches-and-cream complexion glowed against the white blouse and burgundy skirt she wore.

Once again, thoughts of Kendall surfaced, but in a peaceful way this time. Whatever reason God had for taking her brother in his prime, He knew best. Kendall was with his Lord, in that land of untold beauty and wonder. Perhaps at this very moment, he and Doug were smiling down on them all. The notion brought a measure of comfort.

The reading finished, Margo broke into song. "Silent night, holy night. All is calm, all is bright. . . ." As her clear soprano voice filled the room, the others joined in, harmony adding a touching richness to the simple melody.

Uncle Sheldon, belting out a deep bass, reached over and squeezed Tricia's hand; and she jumped in, doing her best to blend with everyone.

"Ah," remarked Wilfred. "That was indeed splendid." His curious gaze darted to the present-laden floor beneath the decked-out fir, his eyes twinkling as he rubbed his bony hands together in glee. " 'Tis time to see what Father Christmas—" he cut a glance at Tricia and winked—"has brought us all." With amazing agility, he sprung up and crossed to the tree, then checked gift tags and began passing things around.

"Let's not be at all shy," Margo cajoled, tearing into her first one with childlike abandon. She squealed with surprise and held up a beautiful hand-knitted scarf with matching gloves from her mother. "Thanks so much, Mum. They're truly beautiful. Now I can throw away my rags."

For just a few moments, the war and all the deprivation it caused were forgotten amid gasps of pleasure and hushed oohs and ahhhs. Small piles of treasures grew beside each person. . . warm sweaters and socks, lovely knitted scarves Isabel had managed to fashion in secret, blouses and silk stockings for the women, finely crafted wallets and coveted books for the men, and little odds and ends Tricia had found in her travels and bought for the sheer pleasure.

But when she opened the final item Wilfred placed on her lap, she nearly burst into tears on the spot. "My very own Bible! How very precious of you both. Thank you so much!"

She jumped up and went to give them each a hug.

Isabel, her own eyes misty, pinkened slightly. "I hope you don't mind its being from the used bookseller's. I'm afraid the new ones were—"

Tricia kissed her on the cheek. "It's perfect. Someone else treasured it once, and now I will treasure it myself. You couldn't have given me anything I'd love more. Now I can stop wearing out the one I've been borrowing from your shelf."

Uncle Sheldon, obviously touched by her display—or struck by a twinge of homesickness for Auntie Maude—cleared his throat. "Well, a moment like this can only be improved with chocolate. Where'd you put that box I brought along, Snooks?"

Tricia retrieved the sweets from a parlor table against the wall and passed them around, delighting in watching each person choose between soft centers and chewy nuts. But when she came to her uncle, she couldn't help laughing lightly. "As lovely as these are, I really don't think anything could improve the wonderful day we've all shared today. I've never been so—"

A knock at the door interrupted her words.

Margo, on her knees gathering discarded wrapping paper and ribbon, looked up in surprise.

"Don't tell me I'm to be summoned to Air Raid Watch on a holiday," Wilfred said, a doleful frown drawing his brows together.

Tricia was the only one on her feet. "I'll get it," she offered, leaving the others to speculate on possible holiday callers.

She turned the knob and opened the door, a polite smile on her face. "Yes?" The smile froze in place, and her heart tripped over itself as she blinked to clear her vision.

The sight of Doug's masculine form didn't fade before her astonished gaze. His lips spread into a lopsided grin. "Am I too late for dinner?"

nineteen

For an eternal moment, Doug and Tricia stood staring at each other.

Doug knew if he lived to be a hundred, he would never forget the priceless expression on Tricia's face when he turned up on her doorstep out of the blue. But then, he probably did look a little worse for wear. He'd been given no choice but to show up, unannounced, in the ill-fitting clothes supplied by his rescuers. When he'd finally convinced the military authorities to interrupt the debriefing and interrogation till after the holiday and returned to the Savoy, the manager had no idea what Sheldon Prescott had done with the belongings Doug had left behind months ago, nor did he have a clue as to Sheldon's whereabouts.

He finally broke the silence. "May I come in?"

"Y—yes. Please do." Finding her voice at last, she stepped aside, her mouth still gaping, her eyes positively huge, like those of a doe caught in headlight beams.

Somehow he sensed a different quality in them.

"I know it's not polite to invite myself," he said, unbuttoning his jacket, unable to keep from drinking in her every beautiful feature. Visions of Tricia's face had kept him going when all he wanted was to give up. It took all his strength not to reach out and take her into his arms. But he knew he had no right.

"It's. . .it's fine," she stammered. "You're always welcome here."

"Who is it, Dear?" Isabel called from the next room.

The older woman's voice seemed to return Tricia to reality, and Doug watched her float back to earth as he hung his coat on the hall tree. "It's all right," she replied. "It's. . .it's Doug. He's come back!" Her voice broke on the last word, and her long lashes dropped over those ocean-deep eyes. She burst into tears.

Tears of joy, he dared to hope. . .only they were his undoing. Forgetting his noble intentions, forgetting propriety and all the tomorrows he'd been prepared to wait for her, he opened his arms. Wordlessly, she melted into them. Sobbing. The rapid pace of her heart found its match in his own pulse.

"I say, what's this?" Mr. Wyndham asked incredulously as he and the others flocked into the room. "A Christmas miracle, no less!"

"I can't believe it!" his wife exclaimed. "We'd quite given up hope."

Sheldon, at least, seemed to take the unexpected appearance of the lost member of his staff in stride. "Well, well, well." He thumped Doug on the back, oblivious to the way he was jarring his niece with each enthusiastic clap. "What took you so long, Buddy?"

Before Doug could answer, the lady of the house took to fluttering about like a mother hen. "Margaret, fix up a nice plate of food for Mr. St. Claire. There's plenty left. I'll go set a place for him. You are hungry, are you not?" she finally remembered to ask.

He grinned. "Starved. I haven't had a bite since yesterday morning."

Tricia, gathering her composure, sniffed and drew back slightly. She gazed up at him with a tremulous smile, even as she swiped at her tears in embarrassment. "I'm sorry. I don't usually do that. I just—"

Already missing the delicious feeling of holding her close, he gave an empathetic squeeze to her shoulder, then cupped her damp cheek in his palm. "I hope that means you're glad to see me," he teased hopefully.

"It might," she returned, a spark of her former poise flickering to life.

"Well, let the poor guy come in and sit down," Sheldon said, shaking his head in wonder. "He's starving, for pity's sake."

❧

Tricia gathered the jumbled fragments of her emotions and let them settle into whatever order they chose as she made room for Doug to pass. Surely she looked a fright after losing control of her emotions before his very eyes.

Then it struck her. Doug was limping! He had been injured! She swallowed hard.

"Here you go, young man," Mrs. Wyndham crooned, taking his elbow and directing him to a chair at the dining table. "I'm afraid you're a bit late for the wonderful dinner our girls cooked, but I'm sure you'll find the leftovers just as tasty."

"Thank you, Ma'am. I expect I will." He eased down, favoring his one leg a little. "I hope you don't mind my barging in on your gathering."

"Not at all. Not at all. The more the merrier." She smiled. "I'd say the surprise has quite made our dear Tricia's day."

Dear Tricia felt her face glowing from the inside, like a light bulb. She'd never live down the embarrassing spectacle she must have made. But chancing a glance at Doug, she saw that he paid no heed to her discomfort. Nor had he seemed to mind her bawling all over him, come to think about it. She just wished she could stop gawking at him.

"Any of the crew make it back?" her uncle asked Doug.

"Yes, Sir. Two guys besides me were rescued by the German resistance. I saw a few of the less fortunate ones marched off to a prison camp. I don't know their names, though, and we heard no word of them."

He gave a nod. "Well, here's Margo with your meal. Snooks, here, can keep you company while you eat. The rest of us'll be in the parlor, thinking up the ten thousand questions we'd like answered."

"I'll get you some tea," Tricia murmured and dashed to the kitchen. After splashing cold water on her face and checking her wavy reflection in the shiny surface of a serving tray, she poured still-hot tea into a cup and carried it in to Doug.

"Thanks. . .Snooks, was it?" He winked.

She couldn't stop her smile. "Uncle Shel has always used silly pet names for me, ever since I was a little girl." The smile faded, and her expression grew serious. "You've been hurt." She braced herself for the details, unable to imagine someone shooting at him with a machine gun or high-powered military rifle, trying to kill him. Doug, of all people. . .

He stopped chewing and swallowed. "Yeah. Even though I'd been coached thoroughly on how to jump out of a plane, when push came to shove, I forgot all about the landing procedure. The sudden stop broke the fool thing."

"Ouch."

"That's what I said, only louder."

She shook her head at the obvious understatement. "Well, I'll wait to hear the whole story with the others. But I'm. . .I'm glad you've come back." As his silver-gray eyes turned to her and lingered, her heart contracted. "I didn't have enough work at the darkroom without your stuff," she hastily explained. "Ned put in for a transfer not too long after Paul left. Only Uncle Sheldon, the two girls, and I stayed around to run the place."

"Then it looks like your troubles are over. I won't be going anywhere for awhile."

Tricia did her best to relax as she watched Doug wolf down the meal, warming under the intensity of his gaze that kept gravitating to her. A million questions of her own swarmed in her head like bees. And the thought that God had actually answered her fervent prayers, despite her wavering faith, both humbled and awed her.

"There's pie," she said, when he'd mopped the last morsel from his plate with a chunk of buttered roll. "If you care for any."

He shook his head and grinned. "I've had plenty. I'm not used to eating a lot. Sure was good, though." That infectious grin spread over his lips.

"Then I suppose we should join the others. We're all dying to hear everything, how you managed to come home to us." *To me,* her heart added. She rose and waited while he ambled to his feet; and when his big hand claimed hers, she was more than glad to oblige. The two of them joined the rest of the waiting family.

Uncle Sheldon jumped up from his spot on the sofa as they entered the parlor. "Sit here, Buddy. And prop that leg of yours on the hassock. I'll just pull up a chair."

While Doug followed his bidding, Tricia took the vacant seat beside him. She couldn't help glancing around at the others, noting that their expressions appeared every bit as inquisitive as she felt, as all eyes turned to him.

"Might as well start at the beginning," he said with a half-grin. "Turns out, I'm not much of a paratrooper."

The men chuckled but didn't interrupt.

"Bombs from our formation had just decimated a good part of Stuttgart, when enemy fighters zeroed in on us. The B-17 I was in took a nasty hit. Things happened real fast after that. The waist gunners shoved me out the exit door, then dived after me. When I slammed into the ground, my leg kinda took the brunt of the impact."

"How terrifying." Isabel shook her head.

"My sentiments exactly—especially when I saw uniformed Germans round up other fellows from the crew. By some miracle—prayer, no doubt—they missed me, so I stayed hidden, as the guys had instructed. I couldn't have moved anyway. I must've passed out, 'cause I wasn't even conscious when the resistance hauled me off to a cave with the two gunners. I woke up with my leg in a splint."

"How fortunate someone knew how to set the fracture," Wilfred mused.

Doug nodded. "The gal in charge brought in a med student from one of the hospitals who was sympathetic to the Allies. The kid knew his stuff. They travel light, though, so he was only able to bind it up as best he could. He assured me it could've been much worse. Thanks to him, it's healed pretty well."

"But you're limping," Tricia remarked with a dubious frown.

"Only because it needs a little more time. It'll be fine."

"You say a gal was in charge of things?" Uncle Sheldon cut in, his gaze darting to Tricia and back.

"Yeah, a brave little farm gal," he replied casually. "Frieda and her two kid brothers brought us food whenever they could. Then, when it appeared the Germans were close to discovering our little hideout, they whisked us through the woods to their parents' house. Their dad is a sheepherder. We stayed in a secret room he'd built under their kitchen, coming up only to eat, for several more weeks. The man was used to tending animals, and he looked after my leg amazingly well, massaging it, helping the muscles to regain strength. Once they obtained false papers for the three of us, they packed us into a truck full of sheep and set off toward Switzerland. That is, right after a group of Nazis happened along and swarmed all over the truck, poking their noses and rifle butts around the animals and the false-bottom tool boxes our rescuers had crammed us into.

"Praise God, they didn't detect our presence, so the sheepherder drove us as far as he could, till his petrol ran out, and we hiked the last bit of it. My two pals were a great help on the trek. . .another miracle I can only look back on in wonder. Of course, from a neutral country there's more than one way a person can get back to England. Which we finally did, a couple hours ago."

"It had to be prayer," Margo remarked, finally entering the conversation. "We've all been praying for you every day. After all, no one had any proof you'd been killed."

A lopsided grin broadened his cheeks. "I had a few doubts of my own, from time to time. But the Denglers, Frieda's family, were staunch believers. Maybe the fact that they refused to give up is what kept us all hoping. Her parents spoke no English, but our spirits were united despite our differences. And whenever they prayed for us, we knew they were talking to the same God and that their pleas were just as fervent as our own."

Tricia, absorbing the whole narrative, had so much to digest that she couldn't trust herself to speak. She just feasted her eyes on Doug and watched everyone's reactions as he related his fantastic story. Meanwhile, her soul poured out wordless praises to the Lord.

"And now," Doug said on a weary sigh, "I'm just glad to be home, where it's relatively safe. I hear the rest of the war's been going fairly well."

"Quite true," Wilfred agreed. "Though there remains a possibility that bombs will again fall on London, now that German forces are regrouping after retreating from North Africa and Russia. We've not relaxed our vigil."

"That must've been one hairy experience," Uncle Sheldon remarked, rubbing his jaw. "Course, we're happy as clams you made it out okay. We'll be glad to have you back at the office, once you're rested up."

"I did nothing but rest for more than two months, but I guess one more week couldn't hurt, after all we went through just to get back here. Then I'll be ready to jump right in. If you saved all my stuff, I should have another camera I can use. My good one went down with the plane."

"No problem. Your belongings are boxed up in my room." He stood. "Well, it's been a delightful day, Isabel, Will. Thanks for stuffing me to the gills—and even more important, for keeping me from another long, lonely holiday. I'll be moseying on back to the hotel now. You're welcome to tag along, Doug." He hiked his brows in question.

"Thanks. I appreciate that. But if it's all the same to you, I'd like to hang around here a bit longer."

Uncle Sheldon's shrewd gaze moved between him and Tricia, and he nodded with understanding. "Well, tomorrow, then. Take care, Buddy. See y'all."

"I'll get your coat," Margo offered as she rose. "Don't forget your gifts."

"And Wilfred, Dear, I do believe a spot of tea is in order," Isabel said, also getting up, her pointed stare rife with meaning.

He flicked a glance toward the sofa. "Right-o."

The once-crowded room emptied out like water pouring

over a dam, and suddenly Tricia found herself alone with Doug. Her heart forgot one beat. Then two.

"Care to go for a walk?" he asked, his eyes questioning.

"Don't you need to rest your leg?"

"Not as much as I need to exercise it. I don't plan on walking like a gimp any longer than necessary. I stop when I need to."

"Okay, then. A walk would be nice."

"Dress warm. It's kinda nippy out there. There's a little snow in the air."

Once they'd bundled up, they quietly took their leave. Tricia cast a glance back over her shoulder at the charming house as she adjusted the new scarf Isabel had made her and smiled. Light from the windows fell in square, golden patches on the new snow. The decorated fir was the perfect touch, its ornaments glistening, its colored bulbs adding cheer. It couldn't look more like Christmas in the waning light. At least it would until Isabel drew the blackout curtain.

Doug held out a hand, palm up, and she placed hers in it, wishing for a fleeting moment that she'd left her gloves behind as she matched her pace to his more halting one and picked her way over the uneven ground. Scattered snowflakes still danced in the wind, swirling about like glitter in a child's toy snowstorm.

"Looks beautiful, doesn't it?" he said, eyeing the inch-deep layer of new white that effectively hid the grays and blacks of the devastation, softening harsh angles. "Like nothing ever happened."

"I wish nothing had. It'll take forever to rebuild the city."

Turning to look down at her, he squeezed her hand. "I really missed you while I was stuck in that cave. It was only my thoughts for you, my prayers for you, that made me hang on. I promised myself that if I ever got back, I'd quit making your life so hard."

"It wasn't hard, only. . .interesting. And I missed you, too. And prayed for you, though I confess my faith wasn't very strong."

"That must be what's different about you. In those beautiful eyes. They're serene now. Peaceful. I couldn't stop looking at them back at the Wyndhams'."

She raised her lashes and met his penetrating gaze. "Well, you did tell me war has a way of changing people, as I recall, making them think about God. And you were right. About everything. I know that now. I know Him now."

❧

Hearing Tricia talking about the Lord in that familiar way sent Doug's spirit soaring. His faith, too, had been weak. Too weak to believe God would answer the prayer dearest to his heart. But He had! The realization took his breath away.

He stopped and drew her to a halt beside him, then raised her chin with the edge of his forefinger, coaxing her gaze to his. "Tricia, I know that during a war is no time to work on a lasting relationship. But I had a lot of time to think while I was lying on that cot waiting for my leg to knit. And I understand now why people in love take a chance on it while it's within their grasp, rather than waiting for the world to become a safer place. No one can be sure of tomorrow, war or no war."

"What are you saying?" she whispered.

"That I love you. I've loved you for quite some time. But with you not having any desire for a relationship with God, I fought my feelings, knowing I shouldn't want you. When it got to the point where I doubted I'd ever see you again, that's when I realized how deep my feelings for you had grown. But still I promised the Lord I'd keep my distance, if He'd only allow me to be able to see you every day, to be near you. To show you what a nice guy I am and keep witnessing to you. Then maybe, in time you'd—"

"I already know what a nice guy you are," she cut in, her luscious lips curving into a smile. "I had plenty of time to think, too. I believe God brought me to England because that's where you are, and He wanted me to come to know and love you. The least we can do is give it a go, as they say in

Britain, and see what else He has planned for us."

"Wait a minute. You love me?" He had to ask.

Tricia smiled, her dazzling eyes shining with heaven's light as she gazed up at him, snowflakes sparkling on her lashes. "Yes. I love you, Doug St. Claire. With all my heart. I realized that the moment I saw you standing there on the Wyndhams' doorstep." She paused, a teasing glint coming to life. "Up until then, I only thought I was in love with you."

Hearing her actually saying the words he'd only dreamed of infused Doug with courage. He drew her to himself, over-joyed that she offered no resistance as he wrapped his arms around her, breathing in the fragrance of her perfumed hair. She raised her slightly parted lips, and he lowered his head and covered them with his own, their hearts throbbing in unison through their heavy coats.

"Sure wish I'd have brought you a Christmas gift," he murmured against her satiny cheek.

"But you did," she returned, a luminous smile lighting her eyes. "You brought me you. What more could I have asked?"

Cupping her face with both hands, Doug kissed her again, more fervently this time. No one knew what the future held. The war might continue for months—even years—plaguing them with constant peril. But God was in control. He would work out His perfect plan for all of them. And Tricia was right. What more could they ask?

BROKEN THINGS

*F*avorite **Heartsong Presents** author Andrea Boeshaar takes us into the world of a woman who courageously faces the failure of her past when she finds a faded photograph of the Chicago cop she once loved. . .but left.

Fiction • 352 pages • 5 ³/₁₆" x 8"

❤ ❤ ❤ ❤ ❤ ❤ ❤ ❤ ❤ ❤ ❤ ❤ ❤ ❤ ❤ ❤ ❤ ❤ ❤

A Letter To Our Readers

Dear Reader:

In order that we might better contribute to your reading enjoyment, we would appreciate your taking a few minutes to respond to the following questions. We welcome your comments and read each form and letter we receive. When completed, please return to the following:

Fiction Editor
Heartsong Presents
PO Box 719
Uhrichsville, Ohio 44683

1. Did you enjoy reading *Double Exposure* by Sally Laity?
   ❏ Very much! I would like to see more books by this author!
   ❏ Moderately. I would have enjoyed it more if

   _____

   _____

   _____

2. Are you a member of **Heartsong Presents**? ❏ Yes ❏ No
   If no, where did you purchase this book? _____

   _____

3. How would you rate, on a scale from 1 (poor) to 5 (superior), the cover design? _____

4. On a scale from 1 (poor) to 10 (superior), please rate the following elements.

   ____ Heroine   ____ Plot
   ____ Hero   ____ Inspirational theme
   ____ Setting   ____ Secondary characters

5. These characters were special because?_____

_____

_____

6. How has this book inspired your life?_____

_____

_____

7. What settings would you like to see covered in future
   Heartsong Presents books? _____

_____

_____

8. What are some inspirational themes you would like to see
   treated in future books? _____

_____

_____

9. Would you be interested in reading other **Heartsong
   Presents** titles? ❏ Yes ❏ No

10. Please check your age range:
    ❏ Under 18   ❏ 18-24
    ❏ 25-34   ❏ 35-45
    ❏ 46-55   ❏ Over 55

Name _____

Occupation _____

Address _____

City_____ State_____ Zip_____